THIS HELPFUL HANDBOOK WILL SERVE AS YOUR GUIDE TO ALFRED G. GRAEBNER MEMORIAL HIGH SCHOOL AND PROVIDE YOU WITH MUCH NEEDED INFORMATION ABOUT YOUR SCHOOL. . . .

What the handbook *doesn't* tell you is how to get *out* of all the mixed-up situations that all the rules and regulations get you *into*—as Julie finds out in an uproarious story of her year's survival at A.G.G.M.H.S.!

"Funny!"
—*Publishers Weekly*

"Amusing!"
—*Kirkus Reviews*

"Entertaining!"
—*School Library Journal*

"Lively!"
—*Bulletin of Center for Children's Books*

Books by Ellen Conford

THE ALFRED G. GRAEBNER MEMORIAL HIGH
   SCHOOL HANDBOOK OF RULES AND
   REGULATIONS: A NOVEL
AND THIS IS LAURA
ANYTHING FOR A FRIEND
FELICIA THE CRITIC
HAIL, HAIL CAMP TIMBERWOOD
LENNY KANDELL, SMART ALECK
THE LUCK OF POKEY BLOOM
ME AND THE TERRIBLE TWO
TO ALL MY FANS, WITH LOVE, FROM SYLVIE

Available from ARCHWAY paperbacks

Ellen Conford

THE
ALFRED G. GRAEBNER
MEMORIAL HIGH SCHOOL

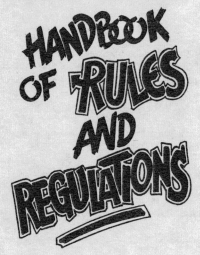

HANDBOOK OF RULES AND REGULATIONS

A NOVEL

AN ARCHWAY PAPERBACK
Published by POCKET BOOKS • NEW YORK

An Archway Paperback published by
POCKET BOOKS, a division of Simon & Schuster, Inc.
1230 Avenue of the Americas, New York, N.Y. 10020

Published by arrangement with Little, Brown and Company
Library of Congress Catalog Card Number: 76-1879

ISBN: 0-671-64388-6

First Pocket Books printing September 1977

17   16   15   14   13   12   11   10   9   8

AN ARCHWAY PAPERBACK and colophon are
trademarks of Simon & Schuster, Inc.

Printed the U.S.A.

IL 7+

1. *WELCOME TO ALFRED G. GRAEBNER MEMORIAL HIGH SCHOOL! TO RETURNING STUDENTS, WE ARE GLAD TO SEE YOU BACK AGAIN. TO NEW FRESHMEN, WE HOPE YOU WILL SOON FEEL AT HOME HERE. THIS HELP-FUL HANDBOOK WILL SERVE AS YOUR GUIDE TO AGGMHS AND PROVIDE YOU WITH MUCH NEEDED INFORMATION ABOUT YOUR SCHOOL, ITS FACILITIES, AND THE RULES AND REG-ULATIONS BY WHICH WE ALL ABIDE.*

"They can't *do* this to me!"

I flung my schedule card on the desk and tried to burn holes in it with my eyes. It didn't make me feel one bit better to hear, all around me in the homeroom, echoes of my heartfelt cry of protest. No one, I was sure, had as good a reason as I to feel bitter toward our new computer.

1

"What's the matter, Julie?"

Mild mannered, sandy-haired Eric Feldman, who sat in the next row and who has never been known to get hysterical about anything, regarded me with his usual pleasant smile.

"They have given me first period gym," I replied, in a voice suitable for the announcement of funerals or executions.

"Is that a problem?"

"Ohh." I groaned at his ignorance. "Of course it's a problem. Look, even if I were athletic, which I'm not—but even if I were, I couldn't jump over sawhorses and do calisthenics at ten after eight in the *morning*. It's inhuman."

"I don't know," Eric shrugged. "Lots of people wake up and do setting-up exercises first thing."

"And people all over England eat kippers for breakfast," I retorted. "Besides, if I have gym first period I'm going to look absolutely rotten the rest of the day. You get all sweaty and your hair hangs—oh, God."

"They have showers," Eric pointed out calmly.

"But they give you four minutes to get dressed," I wailed. "I don't see how *anyone* is expected to—"

"Maybe you could get it changed," Eric suggested.

"Do you think I could?"

"Sure, if you're willing to wait in line for two weeks and you have a study hall you can switch it to."

I shook my head in despair. No study hall,

2

no free period except lunch, and somehow the thought of an 8 A.M. lunch made me slightly ill.

I leaned back in my seat and sighed. On my left, a thin, dark-haired boy I didn't know was smiling angelically as he poked little holes in his schedule card with a sharpened pencil.

He felt my gaze and looked up.

"I think that's pretty much the same as spindling it, don't you?" he asked. Confused, I gave him a weak nod.

"Now I'm going to fold it," he announced softly. He creased the card in half down the middle, then in quarters. He looked at his work with satisfaction.

"And now," he sad cheerily, "comes mutilating." He proceeded to make little tears all around the edge of the card. He whistled as he worked.

I shifted nervously in my seat. It was entirely possible that this was my first experience with mental illness. I didn't know quite how to handle it.

I cleared my throat. "Is there a particular reason you're doing that?"

He emitted a short, evil cackle. *"Revenge,"* he hissed.

I started to turn back toward Eric, figuring that it might be safer not to know this dark-eyed compulsive with an obvious penchant for mutilation, when he said, "Look, one of two things will happen when they put this card back in the computer. Either the computer will have the nervous breakdown it so richly deserves, or a human hand

3

will have to pick out this card for a human eye to see."

He handed the card to me. It read:

GARY GORDON GR 11 HR 114 01224711 1. HOME ECONOMICS 2. LUNCH 3. HOME ECONOMICS 4. STUDY HALL 5. HOME ECONOMICS 6. STUDY HALL 7. LUNCH 8. WOOD SHOP

"I don't even think I'm supposed to be in this homeroom," he said plaintively. He looked around. "This is a *sophomore* homeroom."

I giggled, relieved to find that under the circumstances his odd behavior seemed absolutely appropriate.

He turned back to look at me.

"I have nothing against home ec, you understand, since all I can cook now are hamburgers and an occasional chocolate cake; but I draw the line at slaving over a hot stove *all* day for an entire semester."

"I don't blame you," I agreed, giving him his card.

"So you think my cause is just?" he asked earnestly.

"Oh, definitely. Very just. And I'm sure we're all behind you." I gestured to include the entire homeroom. "One hundred percent."

The bell rang.

"Well, hello there." Gary Gordon patted the seat next to him in the Home Ec model kitchen and I sat down. He was the only boy in the room despite the fact that Home Ec had been an optional elective for boys for the past two years. The girls around us were snickering as if they'd never been exposed to coeducation before.

"This must be a little embarrassing for you," I murmured.

"Oh, no," he said cheerfully. "Remember, I've been here twice already today. I'm getting used to it. The strain is beginning to tell on Ms. Killian, though. The second class was like a word-for-word rerun of the first class—she even told the same little jokes. I think it made her nervous to have me hear the exact same lecture twice. I don't know how she's going to take it when she sees me sitting here again."

We didn't have to wait long to find out.

The bell rang and Ms. Killian strode into the room.

Or at least, she strode halfway into the room, because on seeing Gary she stopped dead in her tracks. She opened her mouth as if to say something, then closed it again, shook her head helplessly and continued to the front of the room.

She leaned against a gleaming formica countertop and clasped her hands together.

"Good afternoon, gir—*students*. I am Ms. Killian." Her gaze was, as if against her will, drawn to Gary.

"Gary, don't you think you'll get bored, hearing the same lesson three times?" There was a note of desperation in her voice.

"I'm just following orders, Ms. Killian."

Titters. All eyes turned on poor Gary.

Ms. Killian, who was young and redhaired and really terrific-looking, bit her lip. That made her look even younger and rather helpless.

"Don't you think you ought to do something about getting your schedule fixed?"

"Oh, I *am*, Ms. Killian." He glanced at me as if only I could appreciate this remark. "But they told me down at the office to follow what was on my card until they got it all straightened out."

Ms. Killian sighed and shook her head. She took a deep breath.

"As you may know, the main unit of this course will be Family Life Education. Family Life Education—or FLE as you'll probably come to call it—covers a wide area of subjects pertaining to living with and getting along with people. We will discuss social and emotional problems, money management in the home, child care and relationships with parents and siblings and—" the slightest hesitation here, "the emotional and physiological aspects of human sexuality."

She glared at us, as if daring anyone in the room to giggle.

No one did.

"Now we're going to be very frank and open here," she said sternly. It sounded vaguely like a threat.

"We'll deal with anything you feel you need to talk about in that area—" Once again she glanced at Gary, but out of the corner of her eyes, as if she didn't want anyone to notice.

"—or any other area within the scope of this course. I'm going to hand out some ditto sheets, which will give you the syllabus of the course and the things you'll need to bring with you, and the readings we'll be doing. Please hold onto these, so if you're absent you can keep up with the work."

She went from table to table with the pile of papers.

When she got to our table Gary opened his notebook and held up a little sheaf of ditto sheets for her to see.

"I have sufficient, thank you," he said, with a gentle smile.

"Julie!"

"Nat!"

Natalie Landis flung her arms around me.

"Oh, thank goodness," she gasped as we scrambled into adjoining seats. "I haven't seen you all day—we have nothing together, not even lunch, and I tell you, I thought I'd *never* see a familiar face again—and my schedule is so *incredibly* awful I don't know how I'm going to make it through a *week*, let alone a semester. I mean, really, Julie, *is* there such a thing as third period lunch? Third period is nine-thirty in the morning! I mean, of *course* there's such a thing, because I was *there*, and there were all those other people there too, and they were actually serving *chow mein,* do you believe it? I mean, I could *smell* it, all the way down the hall. I thought it must be a mistake, until I smelled it, and I got into the lunchroom and saw there were people *eating* it."

I shook my head sympathetically. That was about all you could do once Nat got started talking because she didn't, as far as anyone has ever been able to tell, ever pause to catch her breath. If Natalie wrote papers the way she talked, they would be completely devoid of commas and periods, and her English teacher would probably put brackets around the entire paper and note in red ink, "Run on."

Natalie leaned back in her seat and fanned herself with her schedule card. Her usually creamy skin was flushed and slightly damp looking, and her dark, almost black hair had begun to lose those gentle curved ends which she so patiently encouraged with a curling iron. Nat was on the verge of a severe case of the frizzies—to her, a condition only slightly less dire than leprosy.

As the bell rang, a young guy walked into the room. He wore an open-necked shirt with a dark green sweater-vest over it.

Natalie stopped her hand in mid-fan, her schedule card poised over her nose. "Oh," she whispered, "doesn't he look *exactly* like Robert Redford? Do you think he's in this class? Maybe he's new here. Oh, Julie, isn't he—"

He plopped a pile of papers on the big desk in front of the room and reached for a piece of chalk. Nat dropped her card, revealing a mouth opened in a wide "o." I felt my stomach doing odd things. There was a familiar, disturbing tingle in the skin of my arms. I made a stern attempt to regulate my respiration rate.

Breathe in, I told myself. Hold for a count of five. Breathe out.

On the board he wrote in large capital letters, "MR. CONRAD."

He turned to face the class.

The most gorgeous man I had ever seen on the outside of a movie theater was smiling at me. Well, maybe he was smiling at *everyone*, but he was looking directly at *me*. At least, I'm pretty sure he was looking directly at me.

"Welcome to English Ten," he said. "I'm your teacher, Mr. Conrad, as you can see on the board."

My teacher. My *English* teacher.

He would read my brilliant papers (English, after all, *was* my best subject) and ask to see me privately, after school.

"Your writing shows such promise," he would murmur. "Perhaps I might work with you, help you to bring out that great potential."

He would recognize instantly in me a kindred spirit, a sympathetic mind.

We would read poetry to each other.

I would recite Elizabeth Barrett Browning.

He would quote—with an intensity that betrayed his inmost feelings—selections from Ovid's *Art of Love.*

And then . . .
And *then* . . .
Breathe in. Count five. Breathe out.

Nat and Isobel Gross were waiting for me near the bus.

"Oh, Julie," Nat greeted me, "I was just telling Izzie about Mr. Conrad." She sighed. "You have to see him, Izzie—I mean, you won't believe it till you see him. Listen, if you meet me tomorrow in front of 204 and just wait—"

"I can't," Isobel said irritably. "I'm all the way on the other side of the building then."

"Well, okay, at the end of seventh period, you come to 204—"

We found seats toward the back of the bus, and sank gratefully into them.

"From 316 I have to get to 102 in three minutes," Izzie grumbled. "I don't have time to blink, let alone stop and see this guy."

"Ohh, Iz, you don't know what you're missing," Natalie said, exhaling slowly. "He is the absolute *image* of Robert Redford, isn't he, Julie?" She didn't wait for me to agree, but plunged right on. "Only shorter, he's really not too tall, only about five-seven or eight, wouldn't you say, Julie? But he's got the same eyes, and the same mouth—even the same what do they call it—boyish grin. He doesn't have that little mole, though, or whatever that is on the side of his nose, but except for that—"

"Oh, Natalie, please," Isobel groaned, "you're exhausting me and I've had a perfectly dismal day."

Nat stopped, a slightly hurt look on her face.

"What happened?" I asked. "Could it possibly be worse than first period gym or third period lunch?"

"You have first period gym?" Nat exclaimed. "Oh, Julie, that's awf—"

A cold look from Isobel made Nat clamp her lips shut but she patted my hand consolingly.

"I have Miss De Maria for Social Studies," Isobel announced, "Mr. Gole for Math—"

Natalie groaned.

"Wait, I'm not finished. Mr. Creed for Spanish, Mrs. Daley for English—"

"Oh, Izzie, that's not fair!" Nat cried. "You must have *one* decent teacher—"

"Not one," Izzie said darkly. "Not *one*. You'd think the odds were about a billion to one against having six losers in one semester, wouldn't you? You could go to Lloyd's of London and they'd probably be perfectly happy to insure you against having the six worst teachers in the school in one semester, and charge you a minuscule premium at that. I tell you, I went from one class to another in a *daze*. I kept telling myself after each class, 'Well, look at it this way, Isobel: It can't get any worse.' But it did. All day it kept getting worse."

"Poor Izzie," Nat said. "Oh, I just can't believe it; there must be something you can do."

"There's only one thing I can think of," said Isobel grimly. "Maybe I can manage to come down with a wasting disease, and spend the entire year in bed."

My mother wasn't home yet when I got in. There was mail in the box, so I guessed she had left early for a full day's work. My mother is a freelance photographer and pretty much sets her own hours; sometimes when there's a deadline to meet she works for fourteen hours straight, and my father and I cook while she sleeps for the next two days.

But today she'd left a note saying she'd be home in time to make dinner, so I took a Coke and made myself some cinnamon toast and sat down to look through the mail.

There was a letter from my brother Gabriel, which was the only thing in the batch even marginally addressed to me. I opened it eagerly.

Gabriel was a sophomore in college and I still missed his not being home. It had been worse the year before, when I had to try and get used to it for the first time; but now, although he'd only been gone for a week this year, I found I missed him almost as much as before.

Dear Family,

I returned to find Dear Old Dodd [Dodd College] pretty much the same, except for a couple of ivy-covered halls in the process of

12

being razed by bulldozers, etc., in order to make way for the new computer center.

They're taking over, I thought.

Having attained sophomoricness [although Dad feels I attained that last year, I'm now *officially* sophomoric] I'm allowed to live in the coed dorm. [Try and keep calm, Mother.]

A coed dorm is nice, in that you see lots of girls going in and out of the building, but in actual practice the mingling of the sexes is minimal. It strikes me as the height of hypocrisy to call a dorm coed when floors one and two are restricted to females and floors three and four are restricted to males, and never the twain [quatrain?] shall meet. I mean *never*. [So don't panic, Mom.]

Actually, my mother would not have panicked, but I think Gabe likes to think she would.

We are working on a plan whereby those of us on the fourth floor can lower ourselves out a window on the north side of the building and enter a room on the second floor without being seen in the halls. But there are still some kinks to be ironed out, like how to deal with the campus security force, a surly bunch who would probably take a dim view of people crawling up and down the sides of buildings in the dead of night and creeping into and out of windows except possibly in case of fire. [Don't get excited, Mom. The building is allegedly fireproof.]

My roommate is kind of interesting. He's from Argentina and he's put up pictures of Castro and Mao Tse-tung all over his side of the room. He tends to lapse into hysterical Spanish at the sound of certain words—words like CIA, capitalism, fascist, etc. He has a Sam Browne belt, you know the kind that you strap across your chest and around your waist, which holds about three hundred bullets inside; but I don't think he keeps any ammunition in it. At least, I haven't seen him put any in or take any out. I guess he just likes the way it looks.

Although my Spanish is limited to *buenos dias* and *gracias* and his English, while better than my Spanish, consists mostly of swear words and certain colorful obscenities, we manage to communicate pretty well. For example, when I put up a nice picture of President Kennedy I happened to find, he lunged at it, screamed "CIA dog!" and began slashing at it with the knife he always carries in his pocket.

So I took it down. You see, despite the language barrier, I understood what he meant.

Anyway, registration is tomorrow, and if

that runs true to form I'll have an 8 A.M. Saturday course and four five o'clocks, none of which will provide me with the proper credits for matriculation.

By the way, I haven't the slightest idea how Carlos [that's my roommate's name] is going to take classes given in English and learn anything, but he doesn't seem too worried about it. It may be that learning was not his main reason for coming here.

Julie, some of the girls here have cut their hair short. I don't like it. Don't cut your hair.

Love, everybody,
Gabe

My mother walked in just as I finished reading. "Hi. How was school?"

"First period gym." And, I added silently, I may be hopelessly in love.

"And there's a letter from Gabe," I said. We really look forward to his letters, for obvious reasons.

"Oh, good. I've been waiting for him to remember he has a family. What does he try to shock me with this time?"

"I don't want to spoil it for you," I grinned. "You really have to read it all."

"Well, why don't you read it to me while I make myself some coffee? I am *dead*."

So I read it to her, and she alternately grinned and frowned while she prepared instant coffee.

She sat down in a chair, heaved a big sigh and worked her shoes off with her toes.

"You don't think," she said, "he's really serious about that Carlos character?"

"Well, I don't know," I shrugged. "Who can tell with Gabe? I'm sure he really has an Argentinian roommate named Carlos, but—"

"Right," my mother nodded. She pushed her hair off her forehead and looked past me, at something that wasn't there.

"You never can tell with Gabe."

2. *ANY STUDENT MAY SUBMIT WORK FOR PUBLICATION IN THE LITERARY MAGAZINE "TAPROOTS," WHICH IS THE VEHICLE FOR CREATIVE EXPRESSION OPEN TO ALL WHO SEEK A LITERARY OUTLET.*

The *Taproots* office was a converted broom closet situated between the girls' third-floor bathroom and the east wing stairs. You couldn't open the door all the way because the long table at which the staff worked was almost as wide as the room. Fortunately the staff only consisted of two people; had there been more, they would have overflowed into the hall.

Of course, I didn't know any of this the first time I visited the *Taproots* office. As a matter of fact, I couldn't even *find* the *Taproots* office, although I had followed the directions given in the PA announcement. I walked up and down the hall for about five minutes, vainly searching for a likely door to knock on, and finally went into the nearest classroom and asked a teacher where in the world it was.

"Oh, it's right there," she said. "Next to the Girls' Room."

"But I looked next to the Girls' Room," I said. "The only other thing there is a supply room. It says 'Supplies—No Admittance.'"

"That's it," she said brightly.

I knocked on the door marked "Supplies" and turned the knob.

The door opened about eighteen inches and smacked against something hard. I couldn't push it any further.

"It doesn't go all the way," a voice announced. "Come on in."

I slithered sideways through the narrow opening, holding my breath to make myself as thin as possible. The doorknob wedged against my stomach but I managed to worm my way past it.

Seated on a table (there were no chairs in the room that I could see) was a boy wearing jeans, work boots and a light blue tee shirt with a picture of King Kong on it. His hair was blond and curly, like Little Orphan Annie's, and he was making an unsuccessful attempt to grow a mustache. A lot of scraggly reddish-blond hairs decorated his upper lip, but they hadn't yet grown together in any cohesive pattern.

"I'm Albert Sherman," he said pleasantly. "I edit our humble little effort."

"Hi. I'm Julie Howe. I brought you a few of *my* humble little efforts."

"I *told* you we shouldn't announce that we wanted material."

The deep, gloomy voice nearly made me jump. I looked over to the far right corner of the room. Sitting lotus-legged and slump-shouldered on a metal filing cabinet was a grim girl in a khaki Mao jacket and shabby jeans. Her skin was sallow, her black hair straight, stringy and parted in the middle. She had one of these long, razor-sharp noses and her small, black eyes peered suspiciously at me. She looked like an unreconstructed yippie who had somehow become unstuck in time and landed smack in the middle of the '70's.

"That's our assistant editor," Albert said, "Consuela Fabian. And don't let her discourage you; we're glad to read anything you want to submit. We always need good stuff."

From the corner came a snort of derision.

I tried to ignore it. I reached into my notebook and pulled out the three things I had chosen to submit to *Taproots*.

"There's a haiku and two sort of funny pieces. I wasn't too sure what you needed." It sounded, even to me, that I was convinced of the utter worthlessness of my contributions.

"Two sort of funny pieces," Albert repeated carefully, as if the words hurt his tongue.

He picked them up by the edges, handling them as one might handle a vial of nitroglycerine.

"I'll read them right now," he said generously. "Sit down."

I looked around but still failed to find a chair, so I just leaned against the door and hoped no one would shove it open and crush me against the edge of the table.

Albert read my two humorous essays slowly. He moved his lips occasionally which made me very nervous, because I tried to figure out what part he was up to by lip-reading and couldn't. Once he almost smiled, I think, but it might have been a cramp from the way he was sitting.

I felt completely ill at ease, watching him read my work and waiting for the verdict. The soft, nasal whining of some tuneless song by Consuela also served to set my teeth on edge. It was almost as if she were trying to distract Albert, making sure he couldn't appreciate my writing.

I glanced over at her.

"That's interesting, what you're singing," I said, trying to strike a friendly note. "Did you make it up, or what?"

"Lebanese funeral dirge," she said shortly and turned away to pick some peeling paint off the wall.

"Well," said Albert. "Well."

I waited anxiously.

"You certainly can write."

I was surprised; that wasn't the reaction I'd expected. Maybe he was just one of those people whose expressions you couldn't read. I began to smile warmly at him, feeling my confidence returning.

"But see, the thing is, these aren't exactly what we're looking for."

My smile died. Consuela suddenly quickened the tempo of her dirge, making it sound almost cheerful.

"You don't," I said dully, "like humor."

"Oh, we *do,* we do like humor," he assured me, "as long as it makes a serious point."

I turned that around in my mind for a minute, trying to make something sensible out of it, and then gave up the effort.

"Biting, acerbic satire," he said, "that tears away the fabric of a hypocritical establishment—"

"A slashing, cutting, incisive, scalpel-like wit," Consuela chimed in gloomily. She made chopping motions with the side of her hand, and her voice lingered lovingly over "slashing and cutting."

"*That* we like," Albert finished.

"And my poem? You don't want haikus?"

"Oh, haikus are *nice,*" Albert said earnestly. "I mean, they're a nice, neat poetic form—but see, they're so constricted they don't give you room to say too much. Like your flower haiku." He picked up my poem and read it aloud. Carefully. With absolutely no expression in his voice, like a grocery list.

> *Crocus:*
> *A vivid patch of*
> *Life assurance stronger than*
> *Winter's icy breath.*

I thought I heard a gagging sound from the direction of the filing cabinet, but I can't be absolutely sure.

"That's *nice*," he said (for the third time) "and the 'life assurance' is cute, but it doesn't really say much, if you know what I mean."

"It's haiku," I said defensively. I felt my face start to redden. "It's not *supposed* to—"

"Well, see, that's what I mean," Albert went on. "This particular form doesn't give you enough room for real expression of the violent, passionate emotions that explode in the lines of all *meaningful* poetry. This is just a poem about a flower, if you know what I mean. Con," he said, turning to the assistant editor, "where's that flower poem you wrote?" He turned back to me. "Con wrote a poem about a flower; you listen to this, you'll see what I mean."

Without uncrossing her legs from the lotus position, Consuela bent her torso forward over the edge of the cabinet and pulled open the top drawer. She took out a folder and extricated a battered looseleaf page from within.

"Read it, Con," Albert said eagerly.

Con read it, in a voice deep and harsh with suffering.

Ah, for a flower, just one weak-stemmed
  bloom,
Whose gasping pores are not asphyxiated
By the slimy stagnation of man's progress.
A flower which thrives in sunlight,

Sleeps in moonlight,
And does not have to tremble under
The nuclear umbrella when it rains
Fallout.
A flower untrampled by neo-fascist boots,
Uncrushed by bulldozers raping the land for
  freeways.
(That's progress, sugar.)
Just one flower.

"Wow," I said finally. Weakly.

Con put the folder back in the cabinet and crossed her arms over her chest.

"That's *meaningful*," said Albert. "That just bristles with feeling and life-force. Do you see what I mean?"

"Oh, sure, yeah," I said, not at all as certain as I tried to sound.

"Now, you work on your writing," Albert said, "and I'll bet you'll turn out some really meaty stuff. Okay?"

"Well, I'll try," I promised, taking my three "nice" pieces back and stuffing them into my notebook. "Thanks for reading them anyway."

"Listen, don't be discouraged," Albert said kindly. "You really can write, and when you set your mind to it I'm sure you'll be very good."

"Thanks. Well, I'll see you."

I had to stand to one side of the door to open it and I squeezed out of the *Taproots* office with as much difficulty as I had squeezed in. As I left,

Consuela—at least, I assume it was Consuela—threw a large, heavy object across the room.

I can't imagine what it was, because I hadn't seen any large heavy objects in there, but it made a resounding thud against the wall; a nice counterpoint to Con's explosive, *"Shithead!"*

I don't know why I struggled so to write something that *Taproots* would publish. I mean, on the one hand, I was convinced that whatever I wrote, Consuela would automatically hate it, just as she had automatically hated me. I didn't know whether she had any power to reject and accept submissions to the magazine, or if Albert were the sole judge of what they used, but I had to assume that as assistant editor she had *some* influence over the table of contents. Albert was certainly convinced that she could write poetry, so he probably had a good deal of confidence in her ability to judge poetry.

Besides, I asked myself, why in the world would I want to have anything to do with a publication on which Consuela was the assistant editor? She was the oddest, most hostile and utterly antisocial person I had ever met; she would surely continue to be contemptuous of everything I wrote and my chances of worming my way into her heart—if she had one, and if I had the slightest desire to worm my way into it—were zero.

Despite all that—or maybe, given the nature of human perversity, *because* of all that—I refused to give up so easily. I was a good writer, I told myself. Even Albert had had to admit that. And a good writer writes for whatever publication he can get, at least when he's starting out. And *Taproots* was the only publication at AGGMHS that used creative writing.

My second venture into the *Taproots* office began more auspiciously. Consuela wasn't there.

"Well, hi!" I said brightly to Albert, after having poked my head in the door and discovered Con's absence.

"Hi there," he said. "Glad to see you."

It was obvious that he didn't remember my name, if, in fact, he remembered ever having seen me at all.

"Julie Howe?" I volunteered. "You told me to write some more for you; you didn't like—"

"Oh, yeah, yeah, I remember. So you've got something for us?"

I reached into my notebook.

Just then the door was shoved open and—my nightmare came true—it crashed me into the table, the doorknob ramming me in the small of the back.

"Oof," I gasped in pain. I didn't know whether to rub my back or my stomach first, so I just stood there, tears blurring my vision, and waited for the aches to stop.

"Sorry," droned a familiar voice. "I didn't know anybody was here."

I turned. Blurry-eyed or not, I immediately knew it was Con.

"Oh, it's you," she said. Her voice had the delighted tone of someone who has just discovered a bag of garbage dumped on his front porch.

Well, I told myself gamely, at least *she* remembered me.

That was more optimism than the situation warranted.

"Julie has another contribution for us to look at," Albert told her.

"Peachy."

"Let's see it, Julie."

I gave him my poem. I'd worked hard on that poem, spent days getting it just right, had torn up page after page of first, second and third drafts, until I was sure it was the way I wanted it.

"It's sort of a satire," I said lamely, as if trying to prepare him for the humor he might otherwise overlook.

Again he read it aloud; again, with no emotion or expression whatsoever.

> *Oh omnipotent computer,*
> *Neither masc. nor fem. but neuter,*
> *Giant, manic brain which thrives*
> *On a thousand screwed-up lives,*
> *You who feed on cold, raw data*
> *And regurgitate it later*
> *In some new, bizarre disguise:*
> *Fraught with error, filled with lies,*

And where once were human souls,
Now are punchcards—filled with holes.

"A rhyming poem," said Albert unnecessarily. Possibly he was stalling for time.

"Yes. Well, you know you said 'dahta' instead of 'dayta.' It's supposed to rhyme with 'later.'"

"Oh, right. Well."

Consuela climbed onto the table next to Albert and poked at one of her cuticles with the end of a ball-point pen.

"The rhyming is very good," Albert said. "And you have some very clever things in here."

I closed my eyes, resigned, and waited for the "But."

"But that's the trouble," he went on. "See, it's not really something you're feeling great anger about, so—"

"But I do!" I protested. "I feel *very* angry about computers!"

"See, that doesn't really come across."

"It doesn't?" I didn't know how you could miss it.

"It's too—too *slick*. Too mannered; glib, you know?"

"That's bad?"

"Well, the real emotion, the raw anger and hatred just don't come through. It's—well—it's frigid."

"Oh," I said, defeated.

"You know, rhyming poems are tough, because

27

lots of times they end up sounding ricky-ticky. Ta *da* ta *da* ta *da* ta *da*. You know what I mean."

"Oh sure. Ricky-ticky."

"Exactly," Albert said, pleased at how quickly I caught on.

"Consuela, you wrote a rhyming poem. Where's that rhyming poem you wrote?"

I wondered briefly whether, if I had submitted a poem about lentil soup with garlic croutons, Consuela would have already written one. Better.

The assistant editor sighed heavily, uncoiled herself and walked across the table to the file cabinet, stepping on whatever books and papers happened to lie in her path.

She yanked open the drawer and pulled out the folder. She walked back across the table, plopped down next to Albert and dropped a mangled piece of paper on his lap.

"You read it, Consuela," he urged, handing it back to her. "Now listen to this." His eyes were shining.

Consuela read her poem with such fervor that I thought she might lose control and run shrieking from the room before she'd finished.

> *Hate, kill,*
> *Take a pill.*
> *Drink, smoke,*
> *Choke, choke.*
> *Cripple, maim,*
> *Shame, shame,*
> *Shoot, bomb,*

> *Na-palm.*
> *World, world,*
> *Stop, think!*
> *Oh, world,*
> *You stink.*

Con dropped the poem back into Albert's lap and her head slumped forward, as if it had all been too much for her. Which made two of us. For some inexplicable reason, I had felt overcome with an urge to jump rope while Con was reciting.

"Now there's a rhyming poem," Albert exulted, "which really gets to the guts of the thing."

"That reminds me," Con said suddenly. "You should have said vomit instead of regurgitate." She didn't even look up.

"What?" I asked, confused.

"In your poem. You said regurgitate. Too prissy. Vomit is better. More powerful."

"But vomit makes the rhythm wrong," I pointed out.

"So what?"

I put my poem back into my notebook.

"A couple of shits might have helped it too," Con volunteered, her head still sunk on her chest.

"Oh. Well, thanks for the advice."

"Listen, don't give up," Albert said. "You're getting there. Really. Keep at it."

"I'll try," I said dubiously. *Maybe,* I added to myself. I didn't know if I could face these two again, even if I did manage to write something sordid enough for them to like.

I did my usual contortionist's act to get out of the office and gently closed the door behind me. I waited, just for a second, to hear what Con was going to call me this time.

But there was only silence.

"I'm about ready to give up," I announced to my mother and father that evening. I'd told them the whole story of my attempts at getting published in *Taproots* and they'd listened sympathetically. I even ran upstairs in the middle of dessert to get the haiku and the computer poem I'd written, to show them the kind of thing I was trying to do.

And I repeated as much as I could from memory of Con's work, explaining that I was expected to follow her literary example.

"Sounds to me like they're trying to make a sow's ear out of a silk purse," my father said.

"You know what I think?" My mother tapped her fingers thoughtfully on the table. "I think they want to get people aroused. I don't think they care very much about the actual literary quality of the work, so long as it's controversial."

"I'll bet that's it," my father nodded. "Your haiku is really not quite right, you know."

"It's not?" My father is in advertising; he does mostly public service stuff, like, "Give a Hoot—Don't Pollute," and "Prevent Forest Fires." That kind of thing. (He didn't actually do those two, but he did a really fine one on kidney disease.) Anyway, he's sort of a writer.

"No, because haiku isn't supposed to run over into the next line like you have it. Each line is supposed to be an independent entity."

"Oh, boy, then it really wasn't any good."

"But they didn't know that," he pointed out. "At least they didn't criticize it on those grounds. And I didn't say it wasn't any good," he added hastily.

"Oh, that's all right," I dismissed it. "My ego has stood up under a lot worse today."

"So what are you going to do?" asked my mother. "Will you keep trying?"

"I don't know," I admitted. "I guess I have to decide whether it's worth the struggle to write something they like just to see my name in print, instead of writing what I really want to write."

"That's the problem, all right," my father agreed.

"Well, we'll see," I sighed.

My final submission to *Taproots* took even longer to write than the computer poem. Somewhere along the line in my decision-making process, a sly, nasty idea had come to me. It was the kind of idea that makes you chuckle under your breath, narrow your eyes into little slits, and tap your fingertips together in barely repressed glee.

Now, you might think it's easy to write a bad poem, but to write a really *good* bad poem is hideously difficult. First of all, once you get started in a certain rhythm and rhyme scheme, unless you've got a real tin ear, it's very hard to louse it up. It has a—pardon me—ricky-ticky beat that seems to drive along under its own power and you have to practically work on it with a sledgehammer to dislodge it.

Secondly, it goes against your nature, if you really are serious about writing, which I am, to deliberately turn out something that you know is vile, and that you don't believe one word of.

However, I managed. It took quite a while and a hell of a lot of effort, and three full wastepaper baskets, but I managed.

And in the process I realized that I'd made my decision about whether or not to write what *they* wanted just to get my name in *Taproots*.

"Well, hello again!" Albert, looking as if he hadn't moved since the last time I'd seen him, greeted me warmly. I noticed that his mustache hadn't progressed one bit over the past few weeks. The only difference was that he was now picking what looked like bubble gum out of it.

Con was nowhere to be seen, which I kind of regretted. This time I'd hoped she'd be here.

"Thought I'd try again," I said, handing him my poem. "It's probably not very good."

"Well, let's see," he said graciously.

He started to read it in his usual monotone, but by line three his eyes were alive with pleasure and he began to put real emphasis and drama into every word.

I Hate You:
I hate you, neo-fascist pigs,

For you I do not give two figs,
I hate you, capitalistic scum,
And damn your eyes to kingdom come.
You money-grubbing corporations,
Gouging the poor into starvation,
You giant factories with waste polluting
You military madmen, sieg-heil saluting.
I hate you cops, you too, politicians,
You spend nothing for ecology and billions
    for munitions.
I hate you all to a fare-thee-well
And I hope you all go straight to hell.

He looked up, his face glowing.

"Well, what do you know? What do you know? I'll be *damned*." He shook his head as if he couldn't believe it.

He was still shaking it when Con walked in. This time I had had the presence of mind to stand on the right side of the door, so I avoided impalement by doorknob.

"Hey, Con, read this, will you?"

Albert handed her my poem. I let my eyes wander around the tiny room, avoiding Albert's admiring gaze. I didn't know whether I was going to laugh hysterically or single-handedly tear up the place and cram both editor and assistant editor into the file cabinet.

Wait till next year, I told myself calmly. Next year there will be new editors. Then I'll get in *Taproots.* Next year.

33

"Jeez, that's not bad," Consuela said. She sounded almost human.

"Look at the depth of feeling," Albert marveled. "And the sincerity. You can tell, you can always tell. Your real emotions just *burst* through every line."

"They do?" I asked innocently.

"Oh, yeah—and the rhyming, see, now that's not ricky-ticky."

"It's not?"

"I knew you could do it. Now this is the kind of stuff *Taproots* wants."

"It is?"

"Sure is. And we're going to publish it."

I tried to smile gratefully but my heart was too bitter to carry it off. I plucked the poem out of Con's hands and stuck it in my notebook.

"I have to fix it up first," I explained, at Albert's puzzled look.

"Fix what up? It's perfect!"

"Oh, that's just the first draft. Let me polish it a little."

"Well, look," he said worriedly, "don't polish it too much. We don't want to lose any of those honest, rough edges."

"Oh, no, not too much," I agreed.

I edged toward the door.

"See you soon," said Albert.

Not if I see you first, I thought.

I let myself out the door and stood for a moment on the outside. I suddenly felt no desire to chuckle or tap my fingertips together gleefully.

The whole thing had gone flat. Instead of reveling in the knowledge that I had put a huge joke over on Albert and Consuela, I merely felt deflated.

I pulled the poem out of my notebook, gazed at it as if it were a dish of pureed spinach, and slowly, carefully, ripped it into a thousand pieces. I was about to let the pieces rain to the floor like confetti, when I thought better of littering up the hall, and stuck them in my pocket.

Muffled voices were audible from behind the door.

"Shitheads," I hissed softly.

I turned my back on the *Taproots* office and stomped down the stairs.

3. *IN THE SOPHOMORE OR
   JUNIOR YEAR, ALL STU-
   DENTS WILL TAKE EITHER
   HOME ECONOMICS* (THE
   USUAL OPTION FOR GIRLS.)
   OR SHOP (THE USUAL OP-
   TION FOR BOYS.) *THE
   HOME ECONOMICS COURSE
   WILL INCLUDE A UNIT ON
   FAMILY LIFE EDUCATION.*

Ms. Killian was new to teaching, or at least she was new to AGGMHS. She was very young and wore the most up-to-the-minute clothes. She seemed to be the type who studied *Glamour* magazine carefully before she went out to amass her wardrobe.

As soon as Gary Gordon was gone from her classes (as it turned out, he had taken a shop course last year, and had no room in his schedule, once it was fixed, for the home ec elective), she seemed to be more in control of things, and posi- tively radiated confidence.

She radiated confidence right through the unit on money management and planning for family meals. We budgeted, drew up menus and cooked like mad for several weeks; we had glossy new textbooks crammed with full-color photos of typical meals, charts of the Basic Seven Food Groups and scientific-looking graphs which showed how the American family spent its money.

In fact, Ms. Killian and the textbook made the work of running a home seem so full of constructive challenges and rich rewards that I told my mother I couldn't understand why she didn't want to just stay home all day and housekeep.

"Have you practiced window washing yet?" she asked.

"No," I said, puzzled.

"How about vacuuming? Dusting? Washing floors? Changing diapers? Shampooing rugs? Cleaning ovens?" On and on she reeled them off as I shook my head after each question.

"I'll bet there isn't one photo in that book of how a room looks after a four-year-old has spent an hour in it," she said grimly.

"I didn't notice any," I admitted.

"Well, then." She seemed satisfied that she had explained the whole thing, and maybe she had. I guess it was a lot different discussing the theory of home economics for forty-two minutes five times a week than actually practicing it twenty-four hours a day.

Anyway, we came to Family Life Education ("or FLE as you will probably call it") and Ms. Killian plunged right into the section on Human

Sexuality—almost as if she couldn't wait to get it over with.

We started out by reading for homework the five pages in the book which covered sex. I was surprised to find that our book, which made the delicate balancing of budgets and meals seem as stimulating a challenge as tightrope-walking, managed to make sex sound positively *dull*.

I couldn't understand it. If sex were as pallid, as cut-and-dried biological as that book described it, surely the world would have reached Zero Population Growth eons ago.

The book *said* sex stirred the emotions, was one of the basic drives of all animals, transcended almost everything in your ordinary order of priorities, and then went on to talk about glands, organs and blood pressure.

Of the five pages devoted to sex, one and a half pages dealt with venereal disease; had the three and a half pages preceding VD been the slightest bit stimulating (and I can't imagine anyone being stimulated by the mechanical recital of physiological details and processes) that last page and a half was supposed—I guess—to cool you down.

I began to suspect that the authors of the book were far more turned on by a list of the nutritional components of macaroni than they were by sex. Or that they hoped their readers would be.

I also noticed that there was absolutely no mention of birth control in the chapter. I guess the authors felt that if you were rash enough, or prurient enough, to fool around despite their efforts to turn you off, you deserved whatever was coming to you.

Anyway, the day after we read this chapter, Ms. Killian opened the class by asking, "Are there any questions you have that the book didn't answer?"

I wasn't sure that she really wanted questions; she looked almost hopeful that nobody would raise a hand, so she could zoom right ahead into Sibling Rivalry.

But the hands started to go up, tentatively at first, then more and more, till the room looked like a veritable forest of arms.

Even though she was not the first person to raise her hand, the first girl called on was Lauren Bailey, dark-eyed and serious-looking, with glasses. Not given to giggling.

"What's the most effective method of birth control?"

"I would say the Pill has the best track record," Ms. Killian said confidently. "When taken properly, the Pill is about ninety-eight percent effective in preventing conception."

She started to call on someone else, but Lauren went right on. "What if you don't want to take pills?" she asked. "I mean, who knows what drugs will do to you?"

"There are other alternatives to the Pill," Ms. Killian said. She turned toward the other side of the room.

"Like what?" Lauren persisted.

"Well, there's the I.U.D." Ms. Killian definitely wanted to get on to another question.

"But people have died using the I.U.D.!" Lauren sounded personally outraged that Ms. Killian would even suggest it. "How come it's always the woman who has the responsibility for birth control?" Lauren asked. "How come they don't make a pill for men?"

"Actually," Ms. Killian said briskly, "there is a male contraceptive, although it's not a pill. It's a sheath whichfitsoverthemaleorganandpreventsthespermfromreachingtheeggcells. Yes, Judy?" She raced through the explanation so fast that Judy was taken by surprise when she was acknowledged, and it took her a minute to remember her question.

"Is it true that if you have an abortion you can't ever have a baby again?"

"No," said Ms. Killian, "not necessarily, unless there are complications."

After a few more questions like this, I began to get the feeling that Ms. Killian was deliberately treating sex much in the same way that the book did.

All we were getting were technical details; no one was asking the question—the burning question—that was really on *my* mind.

What was it like? I mean, all this practical information was very useful, and I would file it away in my mind for the time when I would come to need it but wasn't anyone except me dying to know how it actually *felt* to go to bed with some-one?

Maybe they *were* curious, but, like me, couldn't work up the nerve to ask the question. Ms. Killian, for all her talk about openness and frank-ness, just didn't seem her usual secure, with-it self today. I really couldn't help suspecting that the whole discussion was making her nervous. I didn't want to make her even *more* nervous, and I didn't want her to think that I was trying to put her on the spot or anything.

And then I thought, if sex was all so natural and open for discussion, if it were as matter-of-fact as the book and Ms. Killian tried to make it seem, *why was she so nervous?*

Obviously, there was more to sex than Ms. Killian was willing to admit. *Or,* I realized suddenly, maybe—just maybe—Ms. Killian *didn't know.*

According to the grapevine she wasn't married; it was possible that she herself didn't know what sex was like. Maybe in teachers' college she took a course in Sex Education and How to Teach It, and that was why all her information sounded like the textbook.

After all, the other Home Ec teacher, Miss Brady, wasn't married and was teaching us how to be wives and mothers, and Miss Brooke, who retired last year, spent thirty years, I guess, teach-ing a course in which she had no actual on-the-job experience. In fact, it seemed to me that Home Ec teachers, more often than not, were unmarried.

Wasn't it just par for the course to have a teacher teach us about sex without any on-the-job experience?

Wasn't there even an old saying to that effect? "Those who can't do, teach."

I looked up, having lost track of what was going on. Ms. Killian, who had started the class standing right in front of the tables, had backed away from us until she was now leaning against the formica counter, her hands gripping the edge behind her.

"But what's wrong," Sally Farrell was asking, "with making it with a boy before you're married? If you really *love* him, of course," she added earnestly.

"I'm not saying it's wrong," Ms. Killian replied. "I'm not saying it's right, either," she went on hastily.

"You could get pregnant," Ann Boyd warned, without raising her hand.

"Not with the Pill," Sally shot back, looking at Ms. Killian for approval.

Ms. Killian bit her lip.

"Some people," Ann said severely, "don't believe in birth control."

"Then those people," Sally retorted, "better not mess around before they get married."

"Girls, please!" Ms. Killian broke in. "We're not getting involved in moral judgments or religious differences here—"

"But how can you possibly talk about sex without talking about morals?" Ann demanded.

"They are one and inseparable. *One and insep-arable,*" she emphasized, as if pleased with the way the phrase sounded.

"Ms. Killian," Alison Cohen called out from the last table. "Ms. Killian." She waved her hand frantically, until Ms. Killian gave up ignoring her and said, "Yes, Alison?"

"I've been wondering," she began cautiously, "while we've been talking about this, I mean, and—well, maybe this sounds kind of stupid—but if you could—you know, give us sort of an idea—I mean, you know, I understand how it works and all, and what you actually do—but what I was wondering was—well, what is it *like?*"

She looked terribly uncomfortable, and when some of the girls broke into nervous laughter, she shuffled her books together and peered down at them as if the answer was to be found on the cover of her looseleaf.

At last, I thought, glad that someone had worked up the courage to ask.

Apparently I wasn't the only one who was interested, because after the first mild outburst of embarrassed titters, you could have heard a pin drop.

Ms. Killian's brow wrinkled. She hesitated a moment, frowned, glanced at the clock. Finally, in a weak, whispery little-girl voice she managed to squeak out, "Nice."

The bell rang.

Ms. Killian exhaled—possibly for the first time that whole period—and said, "All right, girls. I

43

want you to read pages 111 to 117 on Getting Along with Brothers and Sisters for tomorrow."

Her voice was back to normal. She looked secure and confident once again.

So much for sex.

When I got home, my mother was in her darkroom, developing. Gabe and I had learned at a very early age that you don't walk into my mother's darkroom when the red light above the door is on. She explained it to us very simply, in words we could easily understand.

"If you open this door when the little red light is on," she said, "all of Mommy's pictures will be ruined, and Mommy will get very hysterical and scream and cry."

So I just yelled, "Hi!" down the basement stairs and she yelled back something incomprehensible, which sounded vaguely like, "Momerath's outgrabe, Mabel."

Intelligent conversation on this level obviously being impossible, I went into the kitchen to find something to eat.

There was a letter from Gabe on the table. I forgot how hungry I was and grabbed it up.

Dear All,

First the good news. I have no Saturday classes.

Now the bad news. After buying all my books, I find myself with $13 in my checking account. A small advance on my allotment would be very welcome. Of course, a large advance on my allotment would be even welcomer, but I don't want to be pushy.

Having gotten that unpleasantness over with. . . .

Things are going pretty well. The bio course I managed to evade last year has caught up with me [that computer will track you down to the ends of the earth, if necessary] and it's bad news. I walked in late to lab yesterday, and they were all doing terrible things to frogs.

Now, I had been told to buy a dissecting kit, and I should have realized that we were expected to dissect things with it, but somehow I'd conveniently avoided thinking about that. The kit just looked so neat, with those shiny little knives and pointy instruments. . . .

Anyway, the grad student who was running the lab came over to me, after I had just stood there a while, immobile, looking down at my frog, and asked, "What's the matter, Howe?"

I told him I was an anti-vivisectionist, but that didn't seem to impress him. He just pointed out that the frog was not alive. I asked him if there was any way I could pass this course without dismembering a frog and he said no.

It's a problem.

Carlos is fine, and his English is really improving by leaps and bounds. Someone gave him a copy of *Screw* magazine and he's learned lots of new words.

He's really into guerrilla tactics, and has found a way to sneak down to the first floor without being spotted. [He's a veritable *artiste* of camouflage. I believe he disguises himself as an elevator.]

He nearly succeeded in carrying off a stunning sophomore girl last night, but her roommate raised a terrific stink and rallied the troops, consisting of six girls who chased him down the hall hurling unabridged dictionaries at his head until he dropped her.

He's been sulking ever since, but I expect he'll get over it.

There's really nothing much else. I have my eye on an interesting looking girl down on the second floor. I haven't found out her name yet, but she's about 5′9″ and a snappy dresser. Right through our recent cold spell she wore her track shirt and shorts to class; you have to admire her stamina.

Julie—study hard and get good marks, and before you know it, you too will be receiving all the advantages of a higher education.

Love,
Gabe

"You saw Gabe's letter?" My mother came into the kitchen pulling her sleeves down.
"Yeah."

Suddenly I desperately wished Gabe would walk through the door that moment. I really needed to talk to him, and it wasn't the kind of talking you could get into on the phone, even if I could afford a one-hour long-distance call. And in a letter? Never.

There was my mother, slicing bananas into liquid Jell-O, available, as she'd always taken pains to point out, for any discussions on any subject whatsoever. She'd always answered my questions about sex directly and honestly (as far as I knew) but then again, the most difficult question I'd ever asked her was, "But how does the seed *get* there, Mommy?"

Biology. Mechanics. All the answers about sex I'd ever gotten from anybody—parent, teacher, textbook—made the act of intercourse sound purely like an exercise in logistics.

But maybe the questions I'd asked before required answers like that. Somehow, now that the nature of my questions was different, I just didn't feel like I wanted to ask them of my mother.

Why not?

I wasn't sure. I just knew I didn't want to.

Natalie called later.

She was dying to hear everything I'd picked up in FLE. Her Home Ec teacher was Miss Brady, who was putting off getting to FLE until the end of the semester, possibly in the hope that some time before then an earthquake would level the school.

I carefully closed the door to my room before I began describing the class to Nat. I sprawled out on the bed and proceeded to give her all the questions and answers I could remember.

"She said that the best contraceptive was the Pill."

"I knew that."

"Yeah. Let's see. She said that if you had an abortion it didn't mean you couldn't have a baby later on."

"I knew that too," Nat said.

"She said it wasn't wrong to make it before you're married."

"She said *that?*"

"She also said it wasn't right, either."

"Oh, brother."

"Listen, Nat, the whole thing was a big nothing. It was almost *depressing*."

"Oh, Julie, how could it be depressing? I would have been fascinated, completely fascinated."

"You think so, huh? Listen to this. Someone asked her right at the end, what it was like, you know? And you know what she said? She said, 'Nice.' *Nice!* Nice is for babies, or afghans or bedroom slippers, or—or—"

"Well," Nat said dubiously, "it's nice to know it's nice. Not that I didn't think it *wouldn't* be nice, but—"

"Oh, Nat, why don't they tell us the *real* facts of life, if they're going to tell us anything at all?"

She giggled. "My father always says it's a shame they don't let us learn about it on the streets, like he did in his day. He says they take all the fun out of sex this way."

"Maybe that's the whole point," I said glumly.

"You know," she said, sounding very thoughtful, "maybe it is."

**4. THE ONLY LEGAL EXCUSES
FOR ABSENCE OR TARDI-
NESS ALLOWED UNDER THE
STATE EDUCATION LAW
ARE SICKNESS, DEATH IN
THE FAMILY OR RELIGIOUS
OBSERVANCE.**

"Don't you think," asked Natalie, as we sat in her room making half-hearted attempts to complete our homework, "that Izzie's been missing an awful lot of school? I mean, I know she threatened to spend the whole year in bed, but I didn't think she'd actually do it. How many headaches can she have? Every time I call her to find out why she's absent, she has a headache."

I waited until I was absolutely sure Nat was going to pause for some reply. You have to watch her mouth. Like if you're at a concert and you want to be sure the symphony is over and it's time to applaud, you wait for the conductor to put down his baton and turn around. It's that way with Nat. When her lips meet for more than a split second, you know she's finished talking for the moment.

"I guess if we had the schedule she does, we'd get headaches as often as possible too," I said finally.

"Yes, but, Julie, she's been absent more than she's been in school. What if she misses so much she flunks everything, and has to take the whole year over again? And gets the same teachers!" She was horrified at the thought.

"Izzie's smart," I said hopefully. "She'll keep up."

As a matter of fact, the next day Isobel made one of her increasingly rare appearances on the bus.

"Another headache yesterday?" I asked, sitting down in the seat behind her and Natalie.

"Nope. Zoroaster's birthday."

"I beg your pardon?"

Nat turned around in her seat and rolled her eyes heavenward.

"Zoroaster. The founder of Zoroastrianism."

"You know, it must be the fumes in this bus," I muttered, "but for some reason I still don't understand why you weren't in school yesterday."

"Religious holiday," Izzie said crisply.

"Oh. It's a *religion*."

"What did you think it was?"

"I didn't think it was anything," I said, confused. "As a matter of fact, this is the first I've ever heard of it."

"Well, it's not all that popular a religion," Izzie admitted. "In fact, it's rather obscure. There are only about 138,000 of us in the entire world."

51

"An elite group," I remarked. "When did you convert?"

"When I ran out of Jewish holidays," Isobel said blandly.

"And yesterday was Zor—whoever he was—his birthday?"

"Zoroaster." She pronounced it carefully, to make sure I got it. "Actually, they're not sure of the exact date of his birth. It's listed as 660 questionmark to 583 questionmark BC *or* circa 570 questionmark to 500 questionmark BC."

"But somehow you figured out that yesterday was his birthday?"

"Well, why not? It *could* have been."

Nat rolled her eyes again.

"And your father is letting you get away with this?" I asked unbelievingly.

"Oh, my father," she shrugged. "What's he got to do with it?"

"He has to sign your absence note," I pointed out.

"Don't be silly. Maria can do that perfectly well."

Maria is the housekeeper.

Izzie's mother left them when Izzie was nine. She just wrote them a note and left one day, and they haven't seen her since. Mr. Gross hired a succession of housekeepers, of whom Maria was the most recent, to take care of Isobel and the house. He'd told them all, within Isobel's hearing, that the child was far more important than the housework, and the main thing was to keep her happy.

Izzie had very little trouble managing the maids after that.

Anyway, Maria was from the Dominican Republic and spoke about five words of English: Okay, hello, good-bye, yes, no. That was about it.

Since Mr. Gross spoke virtually the same number of words in Spanish, there was very little communication between them. Izzie, who was in her third year of Spanish, carried on whatever conversation was necessary.

"Nice set-up you've got there," I commented. "I wonder how long it'll last."

"You sound like you're doubting the sincerity of my religious convictions," Isobel said acidly.

"Oh, heavens, no," I protested. "I wouldn't doubt them for an instant. But tell me, besides celebrating Zoroaster's birthday, what do you do? I mean, religion-wise?"

"Well, religion-wise," she repeated sarcastically, "we believe that the motive power of the universe is the struggle between good and evil. Now, there's Ahura Mazdah, the head of the good gods—"

"Sounds like a car," Nat giggled.

Isobel ignored her.

"And Ahriman, chief of the evil forces. And eventually, there's going to be this great war, and Ahura Mazdah will win out."

"There's good news," I said.

"When is this war going to be?" asked Nat.

"Well, of course, it's going on all the time," Isobel replied.

"Just look around you," I agreed.

"But one day there will be the *ultimate* conflict," Isobel said somberly. "And evil will be forever vanquished."

"I don't suppose you want to lay odds on that?" I said, but very softly.

Isobel heard me though, and turned all the way around in her seat to give me a cold, hard stare.

Fortunately we'd reached the school by this time.

For a couple of weeks, Isobel managed to miss one day of school for every two she attended. When we asked her why she'd been out, since surely she wasn't able to celebrate Zoroaster's birthday more than once a year (although, come to think of it, I don't know why she couldn't, considering) she just replied, "Purification rites."

Zoroastrianism, it seemed, was very big on purification rites.

Well, I assured Natalie, when the ultimate conflict came, Izzie would certainly be ready.

Then, one afternoon, I called her. She'd been absent for two days, and the first thing I said when she answered the phone was, "Don't tell me. Purification rites, right?"

"Nope. I was all tied up searching for the elixir of immortality."

?

"Julie? You still there?"

"I'm here," I grumbled. "Where the hell are *you* at?"

"Listen, I'm not kidding," Izzie said. "That's why I was out. I was researching immortality. It's one of the main things of my religion."

"You never said Zoroastrianism—"

"Not Zoroastrianism," she said impatiently. "Taoism. I've outgrown Zoroastrianism. I'm really into Tao. They're big on alchemy too. Why I can't figure out though, since the alchemists were always trying to change lead into gold, and the highest goal in Tao is supposed to be suppressing desire."

"Tried cold showers?"

"Julie, I don't think you're taking me seriously."

"Do you really expect me to take you seriously?"

"Well, *I* take it seriously." She did sound insulted.

"I'm sorry," I said grudgingly. "I guess you just surprised me. What kind of research can you possibly do on an elixir of immortality? You nearly flunked science in junior high when we had that unit on chemistry."

"Oh, that doesn't matter. I mean, I'm not even ready to experiment yet. First I have to read up on what everybody else has tried in the immortality field."

"That ought to keep you busy for a while." Like five years, I added silently.

"Oh, I expect it will," she said. She sounded

55

absolutely jubilant. "And when I'm not busy at that, I'll need some time off to work on my mystical contemplation."

"Oh, sure. Mustn't forget mystical contemplation."

"Well, of course not," she retorted. "How else do you escape from the illusion of desire?"

"Cold showers," I repeated. (I couldn't help it.)

Several days after Thanksgiving, Nat and I went home with Isobel on one of the few days she was actually in school. We made tea, and took it up to her room, although there was really no reason why we couldn't talk in the kitchen, since Maria couldn't understand anything we said. Force of habit, I guess.

There was a new addition to Izzie's room, which I noticed right off the bat; a large ceramic reproduction of the Three Monkeys—you know, "See no evil, hear no evil, etc."

"Do you *like* that?" I asked cautiously.

Izzie wrinkled her nose. "Well, to tell you the truth, it's not what I would have picked, except those were the only monkeys I could find."

"But why did you want monkeys at all?" Nat asked, sitting down on the floor with her tea. "If you ask me, that statue is definitely not your style. You know what would be good? A little—"

"Because monkeys are sacred," Isobel cut in. "That's not generally known; everybody knows cows are sacred, and you can't eat meat, but most people don't realize the monkey is sacred too."

"Sacred to what?" I asked, almost afraid to hear the answer.

"To the devout Hindu," Isobel replied serenely.

"Oh, *Isobel!*" I shrieked. I flung myself onto her bed so violently it banged against the wall.

"Izzie," Nat said, "why do you keep changing all the time? This is so *confusing*. Two weeks ago you were Tao, before that, Zoroastrian, before that, Jewish, now Hindu—"

"You can't keep track of the prayers," I grumbled, "without a scorecard."

Isobel nodded briefly in my direction. "Very good, dear. Very good," she said patronizingly.

At which moment, the door to her room flew open. Mr. Gross, looking like an avenging angel, stood on the threshold.

"Dad!" Isobel leaped to her feet. "What are you doing home so early?"

"I got a call from your school today, Isobel," he said, his voice sounding as if he were keeping it under tight control. "I think we'd better have a talk." He looked pointedly at Nat and me.

"Well," I said, getting up, "I guess I'd better be going."

I glanced nervously at Mr. Gross. He was really a handsome man, but at the moment he looked as if he might—given the slightest provocation—start breathing fire.

"No, stay," Izzie ordered. "I may need character witnesses."

"Iz—" I began uncomfortably. I didn't want to be around during the kind of "talk" this might turn into.

"Then you know what this is all about?" her father asked.

"I have a pretty good idea," Izzie said wryly.

"They told me," he went on, apparently prepared to ignore Nat and me, "that you had missed thirty out of sixty-one days of school so far. Is that true?"

"I haven't got the exact figures." Isobel replied. "But that sounds pretty close."

"Well, were you sick? And why didn't I know about it?"

"No, most of the time I wasn't sick. I stayed home mainly for religious reasons."

"What religious reasons?" he demanded. "We haven't had a holiday since the middle of October."

"*You* haven't," Isobel said. "But *I* have."

His face reddened. "Isobel, I'm running out of patience!"

"Izzie converted!" Nat volunteered. "A few times," she added lamely.

"You *what?*"

"Dad, I have the six worst teachers in the entire school," Isobel began. "Do you know what it's like to sit in a seat for seven hours a day and be so bored you want to scream?"

"That doesn't give you the right to turn into a truant!" he shouted.

58

"Don't label me! I'm not a truant! Every time I stayed out I had a good reason."

"Like Zoroaster's birthday," Nat commented helpfully.

Iz threw her an exasperated glance.

"I'll tell you something, Dad. I learned more at home than I would have in school."

"That's true," Nat said. "You wouldn't believe how much she's taught herself about world religions."

"That's fine," Mr. Gross said, trying to stay calm, "but that's not in your curriculum. I think outside learning is fine, but in *addition* to school, not instead of it."

"Dad, I wasn't learning *anything* in school. You really have no idea what losers those teachers are."

"Then why didn't you tell me that right from the beginning?"

Isobel shrugged. "You didn't ask me."

"Oh, come on! That's no answer."

"But you didn't," Isobel insisted. "So it never occurred to me to tell you. What good would it have done, anyway?"

"I could have gone down there and gotten your classes changed," he said.

"Oh, sure," Izzie said sarcastically.

"Or for that matter," he added, "you could have tried that yourself first, before you decided that the only solution was to play hookey."

"I didn't play hookey! I stayed home to observe

the requirements of my religion. Or religions," she conceded, a bit sheepishly.

Mr. Gross fixed his eyes on Izzie's face, almost as if he were trying to peer into her soul. Finally he shook his head, and for the first time looked as if he might even smile.

"This is really something," he said. "For thousands of years we've suffered persecution, been the victim of purges, pogroms, genocide, inquisition, and still managed to hold onto the faith of our fathers—and all it took to convert *you* was a little boredom."

Isobel almost smiled herself. "Well," she said ruefully, "it wasn't a little boredom. It was a whole lot of boredom."

"They really are," I told him, "a bunch of very bad teachers. I mean, it's not just Izzie's opinion. They have *reputations*."

"So we'll do something about it," Mr. Gross said. "Which is what should have been done in the first place."

Sure enough, the next morning Mr. Gross drove Isobel to school and paid a visit to her guidance counselor.

After an hour-long discussion, during which, Isobel later reported proudly, her father made Clarence Darrow look like a tongue-tied amateur debater, the guidance counselor consulted with the computer, and found it was indeed possible to switch Izzie's schedule around.

With the exception of Spanish, in which Isobel

graciously agreed to stay put, since she was very good in Spanish anyway and said she didn't expect perfection from the school, every class was changed.

They also discovered, on checking her records, that Isobel was running As and Bs in every subject, despite the fact that she'd missed as many classes as she'd attended. She had showed up for all the tests, kept up with the assignments, and handed in everything she was supposed to hand in. In fact, on the whole she was doing better than most of the kids in her classes with more reasonable attendance records than hers.

Which might have given the guidance counselor something to think about, but probably didn't.

5. *FRATERNITIES, SORORITIES
   AND ALL SUCH SOCIAL
   CLUBS WITH EXCLUSION-
   ARY MEMBERSHIP POLICIES
   ARE DISCOURAGED AND
   NONE OF THEIR ACTIVITIES
   WILL BE PERMITTED IN
   OR AROUND THE SCHOOL.
   ALL ITEMS OF APPAREL,
   JEWELRY, ETC., REPRESENT-
   ING MEMBERSHIP IN SUCH
   ORGANIZATIONS ARE NOT
   CONSIDERED APPROPRIATE
   SCHOOL DRESS.*

"That's a very classy-looking pin," I said admiringly.

Gary Gordon glanced down at his sweater, on which he wore a little silver "X."

"Oh, thanks," he said. "I think it's actually a tie tack, but how often do you get to use a tie tack?"

"What's it stand for?"

"It's from the Explorers' Club. I'm a member."

"Oh, yeah, I've heard of them. That's the discussion club, right?"

"I guess you could call it that," he said. "I don't know what else to call it. It's kind of free-form."

"Sounds interesting."

"Yeah, it really is. Last week we had a debate on whether or not there's such a thing as free will and a Catholic and an atheist ended up in a fist-fight."

I laughed. "That seems like a reasonable way to settle the argument."

"That was nothing," he grinned. "You should have been there the week we debated pacifism. We cleaned up the place afterwards, though," he added hastily.

I shook my head. "Sorry I missed it."

"Hey, why don't you come to the meeting tonight? We're doing Women's Rights. Again," he sighed.

"Can anybody join? I mean, it's not like a school club, is it?"

"We do vote on membership," he replied, "but it's not like a fraternity or anything that's restricted to guys. They have open meetings every once in a while, where you bring new people in and then they pick new members from there. Usually members bring people they think would be good for the group."

"Where's the meeting being held?"

"Joan Slater's house. Listen, I could give you a ride if you want."

"Okay, that'd be great."

Joan Slater was the president of the senior class. She had beautiful clothes, consistently made the honor roll, and was in the process of winning scholarships from every local organization that awarded scholarships.

The Slaters' den, which was where the Explorers' meeting was taking place, made it perfectly clear that Joan wouldn't have had to depend on any of those scholarships in order to attend college.

The place looked like something you'd see in a magazine, over the caption, "Lord Tisdale's Library." Dark mahogany floor-to-ceiling bookshelves gleaming discreetly in the light from the fireplace, comfortable sofas, leather armchairs and a large oriental rug, which was clearly old, but not aged. I mean, it was one of those things that you didn't go out to buy, you just *had* it.

All the available seats were occupied when we arrived, so Gary and I, along with several others, sat down on the rug.

I looked around, trying to pick out the faces I recognized. Some people did look familiar, but they were mostly juniors and seniors, and there was no one I was really friendly with.

Gary was talking to someone on his left and there was no one else sitting near me. I was beginning to feel kind of out of it, having no one to talk to and with no one paying the slightest bit of attention to me.

Suddenly I heard a familiar gloomy voice behind me.

"Want some popcorn?"

I twisted around and saw Consuela Fabian looming over me holding a large ceramic bowl.

"Oh, it's you," she said, a statement which I found no way of responding to. I did feel a momentary panic, though, wondering if she would question me about that poem I had promised *Taproots*. But she didn't. She was no happier to see me again than I was to see her.

I had to reach up to take a handful of the popcorn she was offering, since she didn't bother to bring the bowl down to my level. After I helped myself, she immediately made for the other side of the room, to sit as diametrically opposed to me as possible.

As I nibbled the popcorn, which made me thirsty, little bits of it kept scattering out of my hand onto the rug, which made me nervous. I mean, you go to Natalie's room she has this deep, shaggy rug, which her mother actually *rakes* with a rake every week, and you drop a piece of popcorn in there, what does it matter?

In the first place, you could strew a whole box of cookies over that rug and no one would ever see them, which may not be neat, but is at least discreet. And in the second place, it feels very different to eat popcorn on a rug which you know someone got last year at Kaufman Carpets for

$10.99 a yard at a Columbus Day sale, than it does to eat popcorn on a rug that Mr. Slater's family probably hauled over with them on the *Mayflower*.

So anyway, I was conscientiously picking little popcorn kernels off this rug and carefully sticking them into the pockets of my jeans when a boy got up and called the meeting to order.

Gary finally looked in my direction. "That's Tony Lambert," he said. "He's the president."

Tony Lambert looked much more like a jock than the president of an intellectual organization. He was tall, blond and muscular; I hoped he would stand there through the entire meeting and preside, so that I could spend a pleasant hour or two just gazing at him.

"I see we have some new faces here tonight," he said, smiling fleetingly at me and glancing around to share the smile with whatever new faces there were besides mine.

I warmly returned his smile, but he was already moving on to other things.

"The topic for discussion tonight is Women's Rights. I thought we'd start in a sort of general way by my reading this quote from an article about Malcolm O'Donnell, who started a publication called *Men's Equality Newsletter*, or *MEN*."

There were a few hearty "boos" but Tony just grinned.

"O'Donnell says: 'It is common knowledge that there are far more areas in which women are, to put it plainly, inferior to men than there are in which they are equal, let alone superior. Leaving aside for the moment their obvious lack of achievement in such areas as painting, music, architecture and science, we can clearly see that there are many far more common jobs for which they are physically, emotionally and temperamentally unsuited.' "

Someone less intimidated by heirloom rugs than I threw a piece of popcorn at Tony.

"Hey, I'm just *quoting*," he protested. "Let me finish, then we can fight. 'The idea of a woman rescuing a man from a burning building using the standard fireman's carry is as patently ridiculous as the idea that a woman can apprehend, subdue and take into custody a strapping male criminal, with or without a weapon. Even such a mundane job as garbage collecting requires strength and stamina beyond a woman's capabilities. To dispute this is to ignore biological facts, and those women who persist in trying to invade job areas in which they are clearly incompetent pose a grave danger, not only to themselves, but to those very people they claim they wish to serve.' "

Tony looked around and grinned. "That's it," he announced. "Take it from there."

About eight people started talking at once. I couldn't understand how they could discuss anything this way, but eventually Joan Slater's voice rose louder than everyone else's.

"First of all," she said, repeating it a couple of times until everyone else quieted down, "first of

all, if it's true that women haven't been histori-
cally great artists or composers, it's because they
weren't given the opportunities that men were in
those fields."

"Yeah! Right!"

Tony sat down next to me. My hands threatened to get a little clammy.

"Hi," he said, ignoring the shouting that was
going on around us.

"Hi," I murmured. I didn't trust my voice any
further than that. It felt marvelously nervewrack-
ing to have him sitting so close to me.

"Joan! Joanie!" A boy's voice outshouted
everyone else.

We turned to see who it was.

A skinny, extremely young-looking boy whom
I didn't recognize was getting to his feet.

"Bertram Brady," Tony informed me. "Very
anti-lib. Probably insecure."

I nodded.

"Joanie, you're pretty athletic, right? Softball,
tennis, right?"

Joan nodded suspiciously.

"Well, forget about the painting and the music
for a minute; I mean, he said he wasn't even talking about that. You're taller than I am, and
probably weigh more than I do."

Joan's mouth turned down and she crossed her
arms over her chest.

"Well I defy you to get me across this room in
the fireman's carry. You know what the fireman's
carry is, I suppose," he said patronizingly.

Joan scowled at him. "Certainly."

Tony bent his head close to mine. "He's going to be sorry he started this," he whispered. I could feel his breath on my cheek. It suddenly seemed as if all my bones had melted and run together, leaving me with no visible means of support.

"She is one strong lady," he continued. He sounded proud. His face was expectant and eager.

Then I remembered having seen Tony and Joan together in school—and not just once, either. I closed my eyes and sighed. All the glorious possibilities raised by the nearness of his sturdy young body next to my Jell-O-like one, all the promise inherent in his warm breath on my flushed cheek dissolved like sugar in hot tea.

He hadn't sat down next to me because our eyes had met across a crowded room, and he'd found himself irresistibly drawn to me; he'd sat down next to me because in a crowded room, that's where there happened to be an empty space.

I opened my eyes at the sound of applause and howls of delight. Joan had Bertram slung across her shoulders and was toting him toward the doorway.

"Atta girl, Joanie!" Tony raised his hands above his head in a fighter's victory salute.

"All right, dammit, all right!" Bertram yelled. "Put me down!"

I couldn't help laughing, along with everyone else. I felt a stiffening resolve to overcome the sheer animal magnetism of the Greek God at my

right. Beauty is only skin deep, I reminded myself. Under that gorgeous exterior probably beats
the heart of a boor.

"I told you he'd be sorry," the Greek God said,
his head next to mine again.

I urgently wished that he wouldn't breathe on
my cheek if he didn't mean business.

"And in the second place," Joan went on, only
slightly out of breath, "if a woman knows judo or
karate, she can take on the average criminal as
well as any other cop."

"Hey, Bert," someone yelled, "you want to
challenge her on that too?"

Bertram just sat in his corner and scowled.

"All right," said Tony suddenly, nearly making
me jump, "what about garbage collecting? Those
cans are *heavy*."

"Yeah," a girl shot back from across the room,
"and some *guys* can't lift them either. It all depends on the individual. Not every woman wants
to be a garbage collector, and the ones who do
will have to be able to perform like the men who
do. So where's the problem?"

"I didn't say there was a problem," replied
Tony mildly. "I'm just throwing things in for the
sake of argument."

"A male-dominated society," Consuela
growled, "will never permit women the same opportunities as men. The systematic repression of
women is as brutal as the systematic repression of
blacks, and is for the same socioeconomic reasons."

"That's a lot of crap!" shouted George Kalber, who is black. "You women weren't slaves, you weren't forcibly brought over here to—"

"Oh, yeah?" Three girls turned on him at once.

"What do you call marriage?" one shouted. "Women were their husband's chattel. They were owned, just as much as slaves were owned by their masters."

"Are you going to sit there and tell me that you think being married is the same thing as being clapped into chains and sent over to a strange country to be in bondage to a white slave-owner for the rest of your life?"

"*Yes!*"

George threw up his hands in disgust, and turned to the boy on his right, who shook his head sympathetically and shrugged at the unreasonableness of women.

Pretty soon the meeting broke up into clusters of smaller groups, and if anything, the decibel level grew louder. Tony, Gary and I, along with a few others, formed one group, and when I finally managed to shake off my nervousness at having Tony so close to me, I found myself shouting as loudly as everyone else, and being really stimulated by the argument.

Soon I began to have the strange feeling that both Gary and Tony were hanging on every word I said. They both kept looking at me, they both had little smiles on their lips as I got more and more excited. Oddly enough, instead of making me nervous, the idea was positively exhilarating. And although I can't even remember very well exactly what I said, I felt at the time as if I were rising to heights of oratorical brilliance never before achieved.

It was a wonderful evening.

"Julie, will you sign my toilet paper?" Nat asked, as I sat down behind her and Isobel on the bus the following week.

"I'd be delighted to sign your toilet paper," I muttered. "You want a pithy saying, or just my signature?"

"Just your signature. Now I only need fifty-five more names."

She handed me the roll of tissue. "Don't use a felt-tip pen though. It just seeps right through everything and makes blotches."

"Don't you feel a little silly doing this?" I asked. I signed my name in ball-point pen and handed her back the tissue. She stuck it into her big canvas bag.

"Actually, it's kind of fun. You meet a lot of people this way. I don't mind."

"I don't know why you want to join that sorority in the first place," Isobel said.

"Why not?" Nat sounded defensive. "They have those really gorgeous sweaters and—"

"Oh, Nat, that's so shallow!" Isobel groaned.

"It's not only the sweaters," Nat retorted. "You didn't let me finish. They do all kinds of interesting things. They raise money for charity, and have parties with the fraternities and do things together. They even have sisters who tutor other sisters when they're having trouble in some subject. And," she concluded with pride, "they're the best sorority in the school. You know, all the top girls are in it."

"Cheerleaders," scoffed Isobel. "And Miss America types. The Establishment of tomorrow."

"Well what's wrong with that?" Natalie demanded. "They like me and I like them."

"It *is* shallow," I agreed. "They pick people because they're pretty or popular or—"

"How come they picked you?" Isobel asked.

Nat looked hurt.

"I didn't mean that the way it sounded," Izzie muttered.

"They said," Nat replied coolly, "that I was the Sigma Delta *type*."

"Oh, Nat," Isobel sighed. She shook her head hopelessly.

"But I am," Nat insisted. "I enjoyed myself at the tea, and I liked the girls I met. If that's the way I am, what do you care?"

Isobel didn't answer.

"It doesn't mean," Nat went on earnestly, "that we won't all be friends any more. I mean, you didn't want to be in the sorority anyway, so it's not as if you were blackballed or anything."

Izzie just shrugged. "If that's what you want to do."

73

"Well it is," Nat replied shortly and turned to look out the window.

Gary called the following Wednesday night. They had voted on new members at the Explorers' Club meeting, and no one had found me obnoxious, offensive or in any way objectionable, so I was now officially a member.

"Did all the new people get asked to be members?" I inquired idly, not because I was so curious about them, but just for something to say when our phone conversation lagged a little.

"Two others got in and two didn't. Joan and Consuela thought they were too hostile."

I wondered how I had slipped past Consuela's own hostility. Maybe she'd forgotten my name and thought one of the other people she was fighting to keep out was me.

"Funny," I said. "I thought hostility would be an asset."

"Yeah, well I guess they felt too much of it would just make for bad relationships."

A mystery. Offhand I couldn't think of anyone more hostile and aggressive than Consuela, but perhaps it was possible. Anyway, that didn't matter now.

I was in; I was an Explorer. I would eventually get one of those beautiful silver pins like Gary— and Tony—had, and I would be seeing Tony again next week.

Not that I had any real hopes, or illusions. He would have called me by now if he'd been really interested. But still, he was a lovely sight on which to gaze in case the discussion turned out to be on penal reform or something.

After a few weeks I found that there were a lot of fringe benefits in belonging to the Explorers. I mean, besides the fun of taking part in stimulating discussions which really made you *think*.

Although Tony never did show more than a friendly regard for me (and I eventually disciplined myself to sit next to him without developing a nervous tic), it was nice to see the expressions on Izzie's and Nat's faces when he greeted me warmly in the hall. And it felt good to be likewise greeted by the president of the senior class. I felt I'd gained a little status by knowing Joan Slater.

And there were a lot of other interesting new people to meet in the Explorers. I suddenly felt as if I had many more friends, even if they *were* mostly just acquaintances, who recognized and stopped to talk to me.

I persuaded Isobel to come to one of the open meetings, because although she claimed she "wasn't a joiner," I was sure that she'd be so turned on by the discussion, she'd change her mind. Unfortunately, that evening Consuela and George got into a screaming match about the relative merits of anarchy and communism and the discussion sort of deteriorated.

I tried to tell Isobel it wasn't a typical meeting,

but she was so sure her prejudice had been justi-fied there was no convincing her.

"I don't see why," she said, "you have to set up a special club just to have interesting talks with people."

"But, Iz, how do you find the kind of people you can have interesting talks *with?* When you've got a club like this, you get to meet lots of people you can really relate to. You make new friends—"

"George and watshername—the Dragon Lady —didn't seem to relate all that well," Izzy said drily.

"Consuela. Well, no, maybe not, but they're both very sharp. At least, George is," I amended. Even if we *were* both members of the same club, and even if I did feel a certain loyalty to the Explorers and an obligation to defend them against Izzie's unreasonable remarks, I was not ready to stick up for Con Fabian over *anything*.

"I guess they're the Explorer type," Iz said casually.

"Right," I said. "That's just it."

Nat, who up to this point had been merely an interested bystander, smiled sweetly at me. "Like I'm the Sigma Delta type," she suggested.

"Well, no, I mean—" But I stopped in the middle of the protest, because suddenly I didn't know what I meant.

"And they really do have a nice pin," Natalie went on, gazing at the brand new silver "X" worn proudly on my sweater.

"Listen, stop trying to explain yourself," Isobel

soothed. "Lots of people feel the need to belong. It's perfectly normal."

"Which is not," Nat pointed out, "what you said to me when I joined Sigma Delt."

I was beginning to feel really irritated. How could they compare a sorority to the Explorers' Club? Couldn't they see the difference? But of course, I couldn't elaborate on the differences without putting down Nat's sorority and hurting her feelings.

"But you're above all that," I said to Isobel. "Superior to us 'normal' people."

Izzie shrugged it off. "No. Just different. I'm not a joiner. And what are you so touchy about all of a sudden?"

"I'm not touchy!" I retorted.

But I was.

"As long as you're happy," Isobel said, as if I were a child.

"I'm happy!" I snapped.

Well I *was*. Although I didn't care one bit for Natalie's self-satisfied little smirk.

6. *ELECTIONS FOR CLASS OFFICERS WILL BE HELD EVERY NOVEMBER. ALL STUDENTS SHOULD TAKE PART IN THEIR STUDENT GOVERNMENT, EITHER BY RUNNING FOR OFFICE, OR BY VOTING FOR THE CANDIDATE OF THEIR CHOICE. REMEMBER! STUDENT GOVERNMENT IS YOUR GOVERNMENT!*

"Student government," said Eric Feldman wryly, "is a crock."

"Then why are you running for president of the sophomore class?" I asked.

"I have this crazy, idealistic idea that maybe if I get in I can uncrock it a little."

We were sitting in homeroom the day that candidates had to declare themselves as candidates. Eric had amassed the requisite one hundred signatures from the sophomore class and had his petitions ready to submit.

From the next row over, Gary Gordon leaned

toward me and said, "That's probably what all politicians think when they start out."

Eric winced. "I wish," he said mildly, "you wouldn't call me a politician."

Gary shrugged. "Once you run for something, you're a politician."

"Oh, Gary," I said, "that's not fair. Eric's an idealist. He said so himself."

"Yesterday," Gary said firmly, "he was an idealist. Today he's a politician."

"Would you accept 'self-styled idealist'?" Eric suggested.

"Sure," he said. "That sounds about right. What's your platform?"

"Well, I haven't exactly worked that out yet," Eric admitted.

"So much for idealism."

"Just because he doesn't have his exact program all written down on paper yet," I scolded, "doesn't mean he's not—"

"Oh, listen," Gary cut in, "don't forget student parking. If you're going to run for anything in this place, you've got to come down strongly in favor of more parking spaces for our cars."

"I would like," Eric said wistfully, "to run my campaign without once mentioning student parking."

"Now, Eric," I reminded him, "you have to be practical. There *isn't* enough space for student cars and they're always complaining about it."

Not that anyone really expected anything would be done. There never had been enough parking space at the school and there never would be, unless they forbid the teachers to drive to school, or paved the football field, neither of which was very likely. However, it was true, and handed down as practically legendary, that virtually every candidate ever running for a class office had found "More student parking!" a potent rallying cry.

"Sure," Gary agreed. "You have to be practical."

"You know, that's just what I need," Eric said thoughtfully. "Someone to look on the realistic side of things . . . to sort of moderate my idealism."

"Oh, I don't know," Gary grinned. "I think your idealism is already pretty moderate."

I glared at him.

"I do need a campaign manager."

"Don't look at me," Gary said.

"I wasn't looking at you," Eric replied.

He was looking at *me*.

"How about it, Julie?"

"What do I know about politics?" I asked, startled.

"Look, I need an idea person, someone who can help me put my message across to the people."

"*What* message?" Gary asked.

Eric ignored him. "You don't have to know politics. You're a good writer, you're practical and realistic, you're a very organized person—"

"Me? *Organized?*"

But the idea was exciting. To be Eric's campaign manager! The hoopla of rallies, posters and strategy meetings. With *me* in charge of everything. The thrill of sitting up late on election night waiting for returns to come in from the various precincts. The gala victory party, where the campaign manager finally gets the recognition as the Power behind the Power, the person who made All This possible.

Well, perhaps it wouldn't be exactly like all those movies I'd seen. After all, the presidency of the AGGMHS sophomore class was not exactly the presidency of the United States, but still . . . You had to start somewhere.

"Okay. I'll do it."

"That's great!" Eric said enthusiastically.

"Well, well," Gary said. "A powerful political machine is born. And I Was There."

"Really, Gary," I said, beginning to get irritated by his constant heckling. "You're too cynical."

"Now the first thing we need," Eric mused, "is a catchy slogan."

"A Vote for Feldman is a Vote for Good Government," I said, waving my fist in the air.

"Oh, that's catchy," Gary nodded. "Very catchy."

"I'll work on it," I conceded.

"A Vote for Feldman," I announced at dinner, "is a Vote for Good Government."

"You don't say." My father gazed at me thoughtfully.

"Julie's the campaign manager," my mother explained, "for one of the boys running for class president."

"Oh," my father said. "Oh, I see."

"You see what?" I asked.

"You figured since I was in advertising myself, that if you needed any help—"

"Help!" I cried. "I don't want any help! Whatever gave you an idea like that?" I was furious that he should think I'd come running to him for advice. I was perfectly capable of managing Eric's campaign on my own, and I resented the suggestion that I wasn't.

"Really," I said, too angry to say anything else. *"Really."*

"I'm sorry," he apologized hastily. "I just thought—"

"Well, you're *wrong.*"

"A Vote for Feldman is a Vote for Good Government," he said softly. "Hmm."

"What do you mean, 'hmm'?"

"Oh, nothing."

"It's no good?"

"It's a little long, that's all."

"I'm working on it," I grumbled.

I was in my room later that evening, still working on it, when he came in.

"What's this boy's first name?"

"Eric. Why?"

"Just wondering," he said vaguely, and left.

* * *

The next morning, when I came down to breakfast, there was a little pile of notes next to my plate.

"Your father had to catch an early train this morning and left those for you," my mother said.

I examined the pieces of paper one by one.

"Good government begins with Feldman."

"Feldman: A Fresh Face."

"You have a friend in Feldman."

"Feldman: The people's choice—the student's voice."

"Let Eric do it!"

"I told him I didn't want any help!"

"I know, dear."

"You have a friend in Feldman," I muttered, ripping up a piece of toast.

"He couldn't help it. Once you got his mind started working on it . . ." She shrugged helplessly. "Some people do crossword puzzles."

"I *like* it," Eric insisted. "What difference does it make who thought it up?"

We were sitting in Eric's den that afternoon, having our first strategy meeting of the now officially opened campaign. Along with Eric and me were a few of Eric's friends, Roger Capellini, Ted Brewer and Lenny Schreiber.

"It makes a difference to me," I said. "I'm sorry I even told you about it. I thought you'd think it was funny."

"Darling," said Lenny to Ted in a silly falsetto voice, "do you realize this is our first spat?"

"Bet it won't be the last," Ted predicted darkly.

"You have a friend in Feldman," Eric repeated. "I *like* it. It's catchy. People will remember it."

"All right, all right. Have it your way. It's your campaign."

"Listen, you can work on some others. We'll want plenty of posters and they don't all have to say 'You have a friend in Feldman.'"

"I should hope not," I shuddered.

"Who's your opposition?" Roger asked.

"Candy Barnett and Perdita O'Shea."

"Perdita O'Shea?" Lenny echoed. "Who the hell is Perdita O'Shea?"

"I don't know," Eric said. "I never heard of her. Barnett might be tough though."

"Yeah, she might," Lenny agreed.

Candy Barnett was an honor student, vice-president of her freshman class, secretary of a sorority, and had an enormous circle of devoted friends. I felt a lot less secure about taking Eric to the top with her as our competition.

Perdita O'Shea I discounted as a force in the campaign. I didn't know who she was or why she was running for office, but since no one in the room had even heard of her, it was unlikely that she'd amass enough recognition by the time election day came around to be much competition.

"I think our first job ought to be getting Eric's name before the public," I said briskly. "Everybody has at least heard of Candy Barnett, so she automatically has an edge on us. If we can make

Feldman as familiar as Barnett, that's half the battle."

"How do we do that?" Eric asked.

"We can start right out with posters," I said. "Blanket the school with Feldman for President posters."

"And 'You have a friend in Feldman,'" Lenny added.

"That too," I said sourly. "And Eric has to start right in making himself known."

"How do I do that?"

"Tomorrow morning we'll stand right at the front entrance to the school, and you'll shake hands and introduce yourself to everyone who goes by. It would help if we could give something away with your name on it . . ." I looked around. "I don't suppose anyone here has a relative in the button business? Or printing?"

No one did.

"Well, maybe we can dig up a mimeograph machine somewhere," I said.

"And what does he say when he meets all these people?" asked Roger.

"Why, just, 'Hi, I'm Eric Feldman, I'm running for sophomore class president and I hope you'll vote for me.'"

"And if they ask him *why* they should vote for him?" Roger persisted.

"Oh, no one will ask him that," I assured him.

"Listen, Julie," Eric said, "I think before we do anything else we ought to decide what I'm going to be promising to do if I'm elected."

"But, don't you know?" I asked him, feeling vaguely confused. "I mean, why are you running?"

"To change things," Eric said.

"Great, great, but what things? See, that's your platform, and you have to know what it is, and I kind of thought you had something specific in mind when you decided to run." I felt mildly disappointed.

"Well," Eric hesitated, "I do, I do."

"Okay." I took out a pencil and turned to a fresh page on my steno pad. I don't take steno, but a steno pad seems to me the height of efficiency. Even though I do write clear across the red line in the middle, and never use two columns.

"Okay. What?" Poised pencil, ready to take down Eric's idealistic goals.

"Well, grading on the pass/fail system for one thing. Giving the student more freedom in setting up his schedule."

"Good, good!" I cried, writing hurriedly. "The return to scheduling by human instead of computer."

"Okay." Eric nodded good-naturedly. "Also, more guidance counselors. So they can have effective relationships with the students."

"Fine. Fine." I scribbled on my pad. "And more student parking. Don't forget."

"More student parking," Eric said resignedly.

Eric's mother drove us to school early the next morning, so we could be there before the buses arrived. We stood right in the center of the main walk, so that everyone going inside had to pass us. I carried a large piece of posterboard that I'd printed up with Magic Marker yesterday. It read, "Say hi to Eric."

Of course, there were drawbacks to this system; we couldn't shake hands with everyone, because there were just too many people streaming by all at once. And a lot of them just obeyed my sign and yelled, "Hi, Eric!" as they sped by.

But Eric did greet a lot of people, and by the time the first bell rang he was already complaining that his hand was sore.

"When you get calluses on it, then you can complain," I said hard-heartedly.

Another problem with this random hand-shaking, I thought, as we hurried toward our homeroom, was that only sophomores would be voting for sophomore officers, and there was no way of knowing whether the hand you were shaking was even eligible to write your name on the ballot. Eric had to get his name well-known, but perhaps that wasn't the most efficient way of going about it.

Ted and Lenny had been sent to plaster the school with the posters we'd made yesterday afternoon and they had done their job. Only, Candy Barnett's posters were bigger, slicker and cleverer, and generally made ours look amateurish, if not downright tacky.

Whereas I had depended on black and red Magic Markers to get our message across, Candy's posters were lavish and colorful blends of words and pictures, to which your eye couldn't help but drift after the briefest glance at our stark, "YOU HAVE A FRIEND IN FELDMAN."

"Oh dear," I murmured.

"Yeah," Eric said gloomily. "A person could get a complex."

We had just finished up what our school cafeteria whimsically calls lunch when three short blasts on a very powerful whistle cut through the general din.

In the center of the lunchroom, someone was standing on a bench holding her arms up. The noise died down and as the girl turned around to be seen and heard by everyone, I recognized Con Fabian.

". . . TO INTRODUCE TO YOU THE PEOPLE'S PARTY CANDIDATE FOR PRESIDENT OF THE SOPHOMORE CLASS, PERDITA O'SHEA!"

"The People's Party?" Nat asked curiously. "I didn't know there was one."

"There isn't," I replied. "Con just made that up so it would sound like there's more than one person supporting her."

I turned to Eric. "Do you think we ought to make up a party for you to run under?"

But Eric didn't even hear me. He was gazing at the girl who had replaced Con on the bench, the mysterious Perdita O'Shea.

I hadn't seen her before, which was odd, since we were both sophomores and the school just wasn't that huge. But I was sure I hadn't, because if I had, I would have remembered her.

She had thick, wavy hair which flowed past her shoulders like a jet black cape, pale, creamy skin and big, expressive eyes. I couldn't see the color, but I was certain they would be deep blue. She was slim and graceful and looked more stunning in her faded jeans and blue and white checked shirt than I'd ever look in a bridal gown.

"I want you to know," she said, straining her voice so everyone could hear her, "why I'm running for president of the sophomore class."

"Well, she doesn't have a very good voice," I told Eric. "Too high-pitched and shrieky." But he just shook his head slightly and kept his eyes firmly fixed on his opponent.

"I think it's about time we all faced the truth about student government in this school," she went on. "Every year we elect class officers and every year, the only time we see them after the election is in the class yearbook, where their pictures are printed. Do they do anything? No! Do they serve you, the students? No! But year after year we continue this farce of electing representatives, as if it really mattered who had the title of class president, or class secretary. Well, the People's Party is out to change all that. If I'm elected president of the sophomore class, you're going to see some really meaningful change, not only in this school, but in the whole structure of student government!

"I'm not going to keep you from your lunches

much longer. Right now my campaign manager is passing out position papers which will tell you exactly what I have in mind for this school and exactly what you can expect from me if you elect me. I'll be right here for the rest of this period, so if you want to come and talk to me about anything, I'd be glad to meet you and explain anything that my position paper doesn't make clear. Thank you for listening."

While Perdita was speaking, Con was going from table to table with a huge stack of papers. When she reached our table, she dropped a sheaf of them in front of Isobel and said, "Pass them around, please," and walked off to the next table.

Under the heading, "PERDITA O'SHEA: THE PEOPLE'S PARTY CANDIDATE FOR SOPHOMORE CLASS PRESIDENT" there was a mimeographed list of statements. Among other things, the People's Party advocated the abolition of report cards and grades, the elimination of the Student Store, which they claimed existed only to promote capitalist propaganda at the expense of the students, a system of free cuts, where you didn't have to attend any class at any time you didn't care to, with no excuses or permissions required, the establishment of a truly egalitarian school system, beginning with the right of the student to call all his teachers by their first names, the forming of classes to teach political action and the uses of power, and finally, the abolition of student government, a meaningless elitist institution.

Ridiculous and impossible as some of these

ideas were, I was disturbed, because if nothing else, Perdita and Con had succeeded in getting attention. All over the lunchroom people were actually *reading* these things—and even if some people were snickering, they knew who Perdita was, and the controversy she was going to stir up was going to make them talk about her.

We'd have to do something to counter this move, and I turned to Eric to tell him so, but he wasn't there.

I looked around, puzzled by his disappearance.

"Over there," Isobel pointed.

He was sitting next to Perdita, talking earnestly with her on the same bench from which she had been orating.

"Consorting with the enemy," Izzy joked.

I didn't like it. I didn't like it one bit.

"VOTE FOR FELDMAN! HE'S YOUR MAN!

"IF ANYONE CAN DO IT, ERIC CAN!"

With Nat as our cheerleader our small group managed to make a lot of noise. We had balloons, picket signs, and Ted Brewer with an accordion. We'd attracted quite a few people to our Feldman for President rally.

We set ourselves up in front of the flagpole on the lawn near the main entrance, where everyone coming in that morning would see us and hear us. We chanted "Vote for Feldman, he's your man!" enough times so that the crowd was beginning to get into the spirit of the thing and chant along with us. Now it was time for Eric to say a few—a very few—words to the crowd.

"Let me introduce you to the next president of the sophomore class!" I yelled. "Eric Feldman!"

Natalie, Ted, Lenny, Roger and I screamed and stamped our feet. The spectators applauded politely.

"Thank you," said Eric. "I know how anxious you all are to get inside and start the day's grind." He grinned to let them know he was joking. "I just want to tell you that I hope you'll vote for me, and if I'm elected sophomore class president I'll do my best to make life around here a little more pleasant for all of us."

Natalie, Ted, Lenny, Roger and I cheered and clapped. The spectators began to disperse.

I signaled Ted to begin playing the Eric Feldman Official Campaign Song, and Natalie, Ted, Lenny, Roger and I tried to make our five mediocre voices sound like the Mormon Tabernacle Choir.

WHO'S THE MAN WHO SINGLEHANDED
DOES THE WORK OF TEN?
E-R-I C-F-E L-D-M-A-N.
WHO'S THE SOPHOMORE CLASS'S MOST
OUTSTANDING CITIZEN
E-R-I C-F-E L-D-M-A-N.
ERIC FELDMAN, ERIC FELDMAN, THE
ONLY PRESIDENT FOR YOU AND ME,
SHOUT IT LOUD AND SHOUT IT CLEAR

AND SHOUT IT ONCE AGAIN,
E-R-I C-F-E L-D-M-A-N.

Eric and I had quite an argument about this song, which I'd written to be sung to the tune of the old Mickey Mouse Club theme. He said that when you broke his name up like that people would think of him as Eri Cfe Ldman. I said that was silly, nobody would think of that while they were singing it, but they certainly would remember his name, and the song would stick in their minds.

In any case, the crowd that had begun to break up when Eric finished his little speech was now definitely drifting away toward the school entrance. Only a few stragglers remained, and they looked suspiciously like freshmen.

At the very moment I told Nat to release the balloons, which were *not* filled with helium, and therefore did not float dramatically skyward but sort of plopped to the grass and lay there (we'd been hoping for a windy morning), a small band of People's Party stalwarts came marching down the main walk, arms upraised, chanting.

"O'SHEA, OKAY,
"O'SHEA, OKAY."

Over and over they chanted their simple message. Kids began to fall into step behind them, many of the same kids who'd been at *our* rally, and the cry grew louder and louder as others joined in.

"Catchy slogan," Lenny commented.

"Sheep," I growled. "Just a bunch of sheep following whatever shepherd has the jazziest horn."

"Shepherds don't have horns," Roger pointed out. "Sheep have horns."

"Oh, shut up."

Poster on a second-floor hallway: "CANDY IS DANDY." Scrawled underneath, in felt-tip pen: "But Perdita is sweeter."

At lunch that day Candy Barnett distributed, with the help of about thirty sorority sisters, ball-point pens with "Candy is Dandy" printed on them. She stopped at every table, and while her henchperson passed out the freebies, she smiled radiantly and said, "I hope you'll vote for me. I'll do my best to be a good president."

"That's it?" Izzie said, as Candy left our table and went on to the next one.

"With free pens," Roger said glumly, "what more does she need?"

It was impossible to gauge the true support that Perdita had, but I knew that our real competition was Candy Barnett. Perdita might appeal to a small lunatic fringe, but Candy had everything going for her, including a relative in the ball-point pen business. We had to make a crack in her neatly packaged, Madison-Avenue-type campaign.

But at our strategy meetings, Eric was becoming strangely listless.

"The heart's gone out of him," Ted confided to

me one afternoon. "The loser's psychology has taken over."

"Well, it is an uphill battle," I admitted. "But it's not over yet."

"Wanna bet?"

As the final days of the campaign drew to a close, we worked feverishly on the speech Eric was to give to the Election Assembly which was being held the day before the voting. Each candidate was to give a five-minute spiel on why he should be elected, and this was the last chance Eric was going to have to make an impression on his classmates.

With very little help from Eric, Lenny and I hammered out a fine, concise—practically statesmanlike—monologue on Eric's aims, qualifications and aspirations for his school. I typed it up and told Eric to memorize it if he could, but to at least be sure and go over it several times. I showed him where to be fiery and where to be cool and what phrases to emphasize.

He listened mutely.

"You can do it, Eric! You have to have confidence in yourself. We're all pulling for you."

"Sure," he said.

The morning of the Election Assembly I saw Eric amid a small group of people who were clustered around Perdita. She was standing on a folding chair in the hall, fist up in the air, declaiming.

I grabbed Eric's elbow.

"What are you doing here?" I demanded.

"Oh, just listening," he said evasively.

"Eric, you're a lousy advertisement for yourself."

He shrugged.

The candidates and the campaign managers sat in the front row of the auditorium. All the sophomore class candidates were scheduled to speak, starting with the treasurer and working up to the president. If I hadn't been involved, I would have been bored out of my mind, but I was too nervous to be bored. I kept checking Eric every five minutes to be sure he had his speech in his pocket.

By the time they got to the candidates for president I was concerned that there were an awful lot of half-asleep people in the place. The applaus was polite and each candidate had his or her own rooting section who clapped and yelled louder than the rest of the audience, but there was also a lot of yawning, coughing and shifting around in seats.

Candy spoke first. She promised to work for more student parking, better teacher-student relationships, a student smoking lounge and a sophomore class prom. (Semi-formal.) She said very little, but said it well.

Perdita strode to the microphone next.

Eric leaned forward in his seat.

"My friends and fellow classmates," Perdita began. "My opponent's speech is exactly the sort of campaign rhetoric that has reduced student government at Graebner to the farce it now is."

A few half-hearted boos from those Barnett supporters who were still awake.

"These insignificant details which your class officers concern themselves with make a mockery of what could be a real force in school affairs. Student Power!

"So why am I running at all? And why, especially, am I campaigning to eliminate class officers and student government entirely? Because as it is, student government serves no purpose at all, except to give you the delusion that you're participating in a democracy. Well, you're not. You're pawns of an authoritarian, repressive administration, who lets you play at self-government but gives you no *real* say in anything.

"I'm telling you the time has come to change this! We're going to stop playing their game, we're going to stop pretending we're taking part in anything meaningful.

"Elect me and I'll work to get you *real* power, a *real* voice in the running of this school. And then you won't *need* class presidents and class treasurers, and I promise you that I'm asking you to vote me in so that I can make my office *obsolete!*"

People were awake now. Perdita's shrieks had aroused them and she got more applause than I thought she would. Con, who was sitting a few seats away from me, raised her clasped hands over her head.

I looked over at Eric. He hadn't moved.

I thumped his arm.

"Wake up, Eric, you're on."

He sat back and looked at me blankly.

"Eric, it's your turn! Get up there!"

The principal was introducing him.

Slowly Eric got out of his seat and slowly made his way up to the stage.

He stood in front of the microphone for a minute, looking back at the faces that filled the auditorium.

He cleared his throat.

"I had a prepared speech," he began weakly.

Oh no! OH NO! He lost the speech. No, he couldn't have. I saw him carry it up there with him. I *checked. What the hell is he doing?*

"But for what I'm going to say I don't really need a speech."

I'll kill him. I'll *kill* him.

"I've been thinking it over and listening to what my opponents have been saying. And, for that matter, what I've been saying too. And I've come to a conclusion. The thing is, although I started this campaign with high ideals and what I thought were the best intentions, I don't seem to be that much different from any other candidates running for a class office today. I mean, not only for president, but all the candidates, for all the offices. We all seem to sound the same and to say the same things. I just don't see that much difference, or that much to choose from between any of us.

"With one exception."

I am. I *am*. Definitely. Going. To. Kill. Him.

Eric withdrew his candidacy and threw his support to Perdita O'Shea. He asked all his loyal supporters to please do the same.

At last the sophomore class was awake.

At last Eric had succeeded in getting noticed.

He couldn't look me in the eye as he walked down the stage steps and resumed his seat next to me in the front row.

"I'm sorry," he mumbled.

"Why? *Why?*" I hissed. "Don't tell me, I know why. Oh, Eric, how could you? How could you *do* this to me? To all of us? You threw over everything, dropped out of it the day before elections, destroyed all our hopes and plans and hard work, just for a *girl? That girl?*"

"Yes," said Eric.

"A vote for Feldman," I snarled to my parents, "is a vote for O'Shea."

My father looked confused. "New slogan?"

"New ball game."

The campaign managers—even us former campaign managers—were official vote counters. At least, we watched as two teachers and two students counted the ballots.

To no one's surprise Candy Barnett was elected sophomore class president. By a comfortable margin.

Con Fabian, who was not even a sophomore, shrugged.

"Never expected to *win*," she grunted enigmatically.

No one was waiting for me as I walked down the hall alone, after the results were totaled. No victory parties, and no brooding loser to comfort, either. I don't know why I even went to watch the count, except that I was curious.

As I trudged down the stairs I passed a poster that read, "YOU HAVE A FRIEND IN FELDMAN."

Someone had crossed out the "HAVE" and scrawled in its place, "HAD."

7. *ALL STUDENTS WILL TAKE*
   PHYSICAL EDUCATION AT
   LEAST TWO TIMES A WEEK
   EVERY SEMESTER. THE
   ONLY EXCEPTIONS ARE
   MEDICAL EXCUSES SIGNED
   BY A FAMILY DOCTOR.

Dear Folks,

There is no easy way to tell you this, so I'd better plunge right in and get it over with. I had to drop the biology course and it was too late into the semester to get a refund for it. I know you'll understand; I just couldn't cut up that frog, and I was told in no uncertain terms that if I didn't cut up that frog, and the various items of dissection to come *after* the frog, I was going to flunk for the semester.

Carlos offered to pose as me in lab and dissect the frog for me [he likes to cut up things] but since I'd already made myself highly visible to the lab instructor, I didn't think the ruse would work. And they take a dim view of that kind of thing anyway; they call it cheating and have unpleasant methods of dealing with it—they kick you out of school.

I can fulfill my science requirement by taking a chemistry or geology course instead, where you don't have to cut up anything, so that's what I'll do next semester.

I presented Carlos with my dissection kit, to sort of cement Latin-American relations; he was very touched. He ran his finger along the razor-sharp scalpel and murmured lovingly to it in his native tongue.

I suspect that Carlos can understand a lot more than he lets on. He certainly couldn't have learned English as fast as he did. He communicates when he wants to, which, I think, is when he decides he can trust you.

The girl in the track suit is named Marlene Slack, and I discovered that she is not merely a jock, but has a fine mind. She's very committed to the cause of human rights and individual freedom; in high school she waged a one-woman campaign against the school board when they wanted to dismiss a homosexual teacher. [She lost.] She says the whole experience really *opened her eyes* and the more I talk to her, the more *my* eyes are being opened too.

I may come home one weekend next

month; I'll have to see how my work goes. I'll let you know the week before, anyway.

Love,
Gabe

It really didn't seem fair to me that Gabe could just drop out of a class like that and suffer no consequences at all, except for losing a little money.

My father pointed out that a couple of hundred dollars was not "a little money" and even if Gabe wasn't suffering any consequences that didn't mean there weren't any to suffer.

"I don't see," I grumbled, "how come he can get out of doing something he doesn't want to do and I still have to take first period gym."

"It's not a comparable situation," my father said. "He's in college and you're in high school."

"So?"

"You're required to take gym; he's required to take a science course; he has an alternative and you don't. It's as simple as that."

"There's an alternative. You could get a doctor's note saying I can't take gym."

"But you can," my mother said firmly, "and I'm not going to ask a doctor to lie for you just because you want to get out of it."

It was hopeless to argue with them any further (not that I didn't try). They had this weird notion that gym was *good* for me; that first period gym wouldn't kill me and that we all have to do things in life that we don't particularly want to.

"I never realized," I said bitterly, "how puritanical and narrow-minded you are."

"Well, now you know," replied my father.

Finding no help from that quarter, I determined that the solution to my problem would have to come from within myself. The only thing was that no matter how much I pondered the question, I couldn't come up with a solution. At least, no permanent solution.

I didn't have Isobel's ingenuity. It never would have occurred to me to do all that research on religions and to come up with so many different religious observances that required absence from school.

All I could think of were stop-gap solutions.

"Miss Cooley, I have cramps."

"Got your period?"

"Yeah."

"Well, sit out the class then. Go over to the benches and do some homework."

I didn't have any homework, since it was only first period, but I opened a book and kept one eye on it. With the other I watched the class attempting to vault over pommel horses.

It had been almost too easy. I began to calculate how many times I could have my period. Would she even notice?

Two days later I decided to risk it again. I could still have cramps, couldn't I?

"Miss Cooley, I have my period."

"Still have cramps?"

"Yeah; the first three days are really rough."

"Have you asked your doctor about it? You really shouldn't have so much discomfort for that long."

"Well, no," I said uneasily. I hadn't expected to have to go into details. The more I had to explain the more elaborate became the lie. I mean, I did have my period, so I could tell myself that I wasn't actually lying. But having stated that fact, everything afterwards was slightly exaggerated.

"Exercise might be good for you," she went on. "You really ought to check with your doctor. All right, go sit down."

I sat down on the bench again and watched the others leap, tumble and sprawl around the gym.

Obviously I could only pull this caper once a month, but for two days in the same week, which was something. She wouldn't forget who I was now that I had drawn attention to myself, so I was going to have to think up a few other ways to insure as little participation as possible.

But no inspiration came to me for a while, and I suffered through several successive gym classes (during none of which could I make a successful vault over that diabolical horse) that left me feeling *and* looking haggard for the rest of the morning.

The chance discovery of an old Ace bandage lying at the back of a bathroom cabinet gave me my next opportunity.

On the school bus I wound it around my foot and ankle, forcing my shoe back on (which wasn't easy since my foot was at least a size bigger with the bandage) and limped into school.

Iz and Nat thought it looked pretty convincing, but I was not too confident about Miss Cooley's reaction to my disability.

I hobbled into the gym trying to look sincerely pained, but simultaneously brave. I didn't want to ham up the limp, but on the other hand, I didn't want to appear brave enough to overcome my handicap and take the class.

Unfortunately Miss Cooley couldn't see the bandage because my jeans covered it, so I had to pull them up a little to point it out to her, which wasn't as subtle as I would have liked.

"I sprained it."

"Doing what?" She seemed startled. It was plain that by now she had typed me—correctly— as the sort of person who never does anything more strenuous than coring an apple.

Thinking quickly—I'd somehow neglected to plan for this question—I replied, "On the stairs. At home. Missed a step."

"Do you have a note from your mother?"

"No," I said blankly, trying to convey the impression that what with my bandage and my limp it had never occurred to me that she'd need further proof that I was crippled.

She gave me a long, hard stare. "All right," she said finally. "Go sit down."

The sprained ankle was good for two classes. (I'm a slow healer.) And a week later it was time for me to get my period again.

However the week that I had my period Miss Cooley suddenly became less compassionate. She developed suspicions.

When I tried to sit out the class for the second time that week she frowned and shook her head.

"Without a doctor's note I don't think I can let you miss any more classes I think the exercise might do you good. If you're really that uncomfortable, you ought to have a check-up."

I was filled with resentment over her attitude as I slouched toward the locker room. How did she know how much I was suffering? How could she take it upon herself to force me into physical activity that might very well—considering my condition—be detrimental to my health?

I was so angry and upset over having lost my alibi that I nearly forgot that I wasn't really riddled with pain. For all she knew I was suffering greatly, but did she care? Did she sympathize? The woman had no heart.

Although I had told myself that the solution to my problem had to come from my own resources it certainly seemed to me that Isobel was one of my resources. I mean, you can't be too rigid about these things. If you have a friend with an acute mind and a fine brain, it would be foolish not to let her help you out.

"Well," said Iz, after I had laid the problem in her lap. "Well." She frowned.

"Please, Iz, you've got to think of something. I'm really getting desperate."

"You know," she mused, "if you were to break

your leg and have to wear a cast for six weeks ...
but I don't suppose you'd want to—"

"No," I said firmly. "I wouldn't."

"Oh, well, it was just a thought." She sat back
on her bed and closed her eyes. She stayed that
way for some time, until I began to suspect she
had fallen asleep.

"Iz?"

"I'm working on it."

I sighed and looked around the room. It didn't
look any different than the last time I had looked
around it, so I contemplated my fingernails. They
didn't look any different, either.

"You don't," Isobel said abruptly, "have any
particular hangups about changing into a gym
suit with a locker room full of people, do you?"

"No."

"Too bad. It was a nice idea." She closed her
eyes again.

"I suppose," she said a little while later, "getting pregnant would be a little drastic."

"Yeah, just a bit." I wondered how much
Isobel was going to be able to help me.

"I was only kidding," she muttered.

At last she opened her eyes again and fixed
them gravely on mine. "You know what I think?"

"What?" I asked expectantly.

"I think you better resign yourself to taking
this class."

"Oh, Izzie, I counted on you!"

"I'm sorry," she said earnestly, "but I don't see
that there's anything else you can do, short of

getting yourself suspended. Look, I sympathize, but we all have to take gym. You're not the only one in the first period, you know."

"Oh, thanks a lot."

"I can't help it, Julie. I just don't see any other options. You tried talking to your parents honestly, you've run out of fake excuses, you can't get your schedule changed, what is there left?"

"I thought *you'd* come up with that," I sighed. "You were my last resort."

"I'm sorry," she repeated. "I tried."

"I know you did. Listen, I'd better get going."

"Why don't you stay a while? It's early."

"I can't," I said sullenly. "I have to go home and wash my stupid gym suit."

Which gave me an idea.

"I forgot my gym suit, Miss Cooley."

"You realize," she said darkly, "that will count against your grade?"

"I know." I tried to look concerned. Who cared what my grade in gym was?

"Your sneakers this time?" she asked skeptically. "I see. Are you aware that coming unprepared three times in one marking period means an automatic 'F'."

"No," I gulped. "Actually I wasn't."

I didn't care if I got a "D" in gym, but the horrible notion suddenly crossed my mind that if I flunked I might have to take it over, although I wasn't really clear on that point, because since you have to take it every semester I didn't know when they'd make me take it over. Could they hold up my diploma? Would I—hideous thought —have to double up and take *two* periods of gym in one semester? It made me queasy just contemplating the prospect.

"As a matter of fact," she continued, glancing at her record book, "you're already close to failing. You've missed nine classes, your attitude is certainly not what I'd call cooperative, and when we actually do have the pleasure of your company in our class, you seem a most unwilling, unenthusiastic participant."

I wonder what gave her that idea?

"Failure notices go home at the end of next week you know," she said ominously.

I swallowed hard.

"I'll try to do better," I whispered.

"See that you do."

"Let's go, let's go!" I shouted. "We can get 'em! We're not down yet!" I clapped my hands together and slapped Dawn Fleishman on the shoulder. "Your serve, Dawn!"

We were losing 9-0 in volleyball. I had blown my serve, and, in fact, muffed every shot but one that had come my way. I was hoping, though, that Miss Cooley was noticing my extraordinary enthusiasm and team spirit, which should more than make up for my total ineptitude.

"You don't have to tell everyone whose serve it is," Dawn growled, stepping back to the service line. "And I wish to hell you'd shut up for two seconds."

If I'd cared about the dumb game I might have been hurt, but as it was, I just winked.

"Pulling my grade up," I whispered conspiratorially. "Just ignore me."

She nodded. "I get you. Okay, but you're getting pretty hard to ignore."

She served. The ball sailed over the net and was returned, straight at me. I managed to knock it toward a girl in the first row, who spiked it.

"Nice going, Clare," I shrieked. "Our first point."

"Great pass, Julie," Dawn shouted, with a sidewards glance at Miss Cooley. I smiled gratefully and Dawn winked back at me.

I was absolutely unbearable in gym for the next few weeks. I was so gung ho, such a team player, I practically made me sick to my stomach.

I kept my sneakers dazzling with a twice weekly application of white shoe polish. The sneakers soon had all the flexibility of a redwood picnic table, but comfort was not high on my list of priorities.

I took my jaundice-yellow gym suit home with me after every gym day and threw it in the wash. Ordinarily I would have just snatched it out of the drier and stuffed it into a big bag. But these were not ordinary times. So I spray-starched it and ironed it until it was stiff enough to stand up by itself; I was probably the only person in

AGGMHS to carry her gym suit to school on a hanger.

The remainder of the marking period continued to be devoted to volleyball. Although I never had made it over that pommel horse, I could occasionally smack a volleyball (when I didn't duck) and even when I missed the ball, the team sport gave me the opportunity to exhort my teammates to outdo our opponents, to encourage our players with my constant cheerleading and to generally shock everyone with my sudden attack of acute athleticism.

And no matter how thick I laid it on, it wasn't too thick for old Cooley. I think she marveled at my change in attitude—I actually got a smile from her once—but was not going to look a gift horse in the mouth.

I felt like a first-class phony. Well, I *was* a first-class phony, but, I told myself, if this was how you had to play the game, I'd play the game.

And you know, it's an odd thing; I've read that people can really psych themselves up to learn to like doing things they once wouldn't do, and that the more they act like they're enjoying themselves the more they truly do enjoy themselves, eventually.

So, hard as it is to believe, I managed to pull a "C+" in gym for the marking period . . . and continued to hate every lousy minute of it.

8. *NO DEMONSTRATIONS OF ANY KIND WILL BE HELD IN SCHOOL OR ON SCHOOL GROUNDS.*

"It looks like they really mean it this time," my father said grimly.

"They certainly do," I agreed, bouncing down the stairs. I had just completed my homework, including a perfectly stupendous composition for English, which would make Mr. Conrad finally sit up and notice me, and turn my glorious dreams into reality.

"Indubitably," I went on. *"Sans doute."*

He looked up from the newspaper.

"Do you have any idea what I'm talking about?"

"Not the foggiest," I trilled, practically dancing into the living room.

"Why," he said, turning to my mother, "do I suddenly get the feeling I'm a passenger on the Good Ship *Lollipop?"*

My mother just grinned and shrugged her shoulders.

"Goodness, a person can't win around here," I chided. "Half the time you're asking why I'm so quiet and mopy. Now that I'm cheerful and a joy to be with you're complaining." I sat down next to him on the couch.

"I don't remember the last time I asked why you were mopy. And I'm not complaining."

"Anyway," I said briskly, "who really means what?"

"It looks like there's going to be a teachers' strike. Tomorrow."

"What?"

My face fell. Presto changeo . . . my beautiful mood was gone.

"They can't do that!" I cried. "I didn't really believe they were actually going to do it."

"I think the Good Ship *Lollipop* just capsized," my mother remarked.

"You don't mean this is the first you've heard about it?" my father asked me.

"Oh, of course not. There were *rumors*." I demonstrated with a careless flip of my hand what I thought about rumors.

"They don't sound like rumors anymore," my father said.

I felt suddenly as low as I'd felt high just moments before.

Simply stated, the situation was this: I had discovered, over a period of weeks, that my entire day was structured around English class. I looked forward to it from the time I got to school till the time I sat down at my desk in Mr. Conrad's room. During the forty-two minutes I was there, I hung on his every word, volunteered to answer virtually every question, and shivered when he called my name. When the bell rang, I retained a warm glow as I left the room and proceeded to my next class, and the warm glow and the memory of his gorgeous face stayed with me for the rest of the day.

Two days when he was out sick were two ruined days for me; I was grouchy, irritable, and sulky until he returned. In fact, I suffered withdrawal symptoms. That was when it became obvious to me that I absolutely required regular doses of Mr. Conrad to keep me going. I had all the symptoms of an addict.

How could I get along without my daily English class?

How long would the strike last? Could I make it?

Sunk in gloom, I gazed vacantly down at the rug.

". . . think she ought to go?" my mother was saying.

"I don't know. What do you think?"

"I don't know either. You don't suppose there'll be trouble?"

I looked up. "Trouble about what?"

"Trouble at school. We're wondering if you should stay home tomorrow."

"Oh, I don't know," I said glumly.

"They'll just be picketing," my father said. "I don't see why there should be any trouble. Not with the kids, anyway."

Picketing! I brightened up. Mr. Conrad would be marching back and forth in front of the school with a picket sign. Perhaps I could bring him coffee. Or a sandwich. Or walk along with him, demonstrating my sympathy for his cause. He probably had very good reasons for striking. He was surely underpaid. They couldn't possibly pay a man like Mr. Conrad enough. Why, just think of what he could earn in Hollywood.

Sure enough, the following morning when the bus pulled up in front of the school there was a bunch of teachers striding back and forth along the sidewalk with picket signs. The bus driver stopped across the street instead of pulling into the circular drive in front as he usually does.

"Okay, everybody out," he announced.

"Why here?" several people asked curiously.

"You kids can cross a picket line if you want to," he said self-righteously, "but I ain't never, and I'm not about to start now."

"Boy," grumbled Nat, "if you ask him to let you off one block nearer your house he gets hysterical and says bus company rules; they could get sued if you tripped going out the door at an unscheduled stop. All of a sudden he makes his own rules."

"Really, Nat," said Izzie, "it's only across the street."

"It's not the distance, it's the principle of the thing."

"Do you think they'll try to stop us from going into the school?" I asked, suddenly feeling slightly nervous.

"No, look at all the other kids going in," Iz pointed out.

I didn't see Mr. Conrad anywhere. As we crossed the street I could hear the teachers chanting.

"NO RAISE, NO WORK! NO RAISE, NO WORK!"

I waved at Ms. Killian as we passed her. She dipped her picket sign in greeting. It read, "All we ask is a living wage."

"Are you the only ones on strike?" Iz asked her.

"Oh, no," she said cheerfully. "The strike is one hundred percent effective."

"So who's going to teach us?" Nat mumbled.

"How come the picket line's so small?" asked Iz.

"We're going to take turns," Ms. Killian explained. "One hour shifts all day."

Just my luck, I thought gloomily. Mr. Conrad would be here when I was inside the building and I'd never get a chance to see him.

I sighed as we went into the school. I wondered why we were here at all.

A few hours later I was even more puzzled as to the reasoning behind keeping us in school. I had just finished my fourth study hall of the day. Normally I would be flying down the hall to English class now. Instead I was bored, disgusted and angry.

Secretaries and PTA members were manning the classes and since they weren't prepared to teach anything all they could do was announce that for today, the class was a study hall. However, since no one was teaching anything, we didn't have anything to study, there were no homework assignments, and only a few foresighted people had thought to bring books with them to read.

As if to compensate for not being able to teach anything, these stand-ins were very big on "maintaining order." What else was there for them to do?

So I trudged into English class, disheartened and determined to get my parents to let me stay home for the duration of the strike. I could certainly learn more at home than I could in school, what with the current situation.

I slumped into my seat next to Nat.

She started to say something but the balding man at Mr. Conrad's desk scowled at the class, as if to let us know he was not to be trifled with.

"Guidance counselor," Nat muttered.

This was what I got in place of Mr. Conrad.

I sighed heavily.

"I think," he said, as if it had taken hours of careful planning to come up with the idea, "that we will have a study hall."

At three o'clock, when we left school, the crowd of people in front had grown bigger. There were several policemen standing around keeping an eye on things and the picket line had swelled.

I looked for Mr. Conrad and spotted him wearing a turtleneck sweater and CPO jacket over jeans. He looked more like a student than a teacher. I stood on the sidewalk for a minute, hoping he'd see me and come over to ask who'd taken his class.

He didn't seem to realize I was there, so I kind of ambled toward him, trying to look casual. He was marching in my direction, carrying a sign that said, "A Fair Deal for Teachers."

"Hi, Mr. Conrad."

"Oh, hi there." I fell into step beside him.

"How's it going?" I asked.

"Too early to tell. I think it might be a long haul, though."

I groaned to myself.

"Well, I hope you win."

"Thanks."

At least, I thought as I went toward my bus, at least I had *seen* him.

The only good thing about the strike was that we didn't have to have gym. I managed to get my parents to let me stay out a couple of days because a lot of other kids were staying out too. It seemed senseless to go and sit there for six hours doing nothing.

By the seventh day of the strike things had changed.

When I got to school that day there was a large crowd of kids with picket signs of their own standing on one side of the entrance, separated by a slew of cops from the teachers picketing on the other side.

Standing with the teachers was a cluster of kids

who were waving clenched fists and shouting at the counter-pickets.

And a third group, much smaller, with Con Fabian apparently acting as ringleader, was marching toward the two opposing factions.

"I think I'll just turn around and go home," Nat said firmly.

"No, wait," said Iz. "Let's see what's happening."

The kids with the teachers carried signs like, "Students for a Fair Shake," and "Support Our Teachers." They were chanting something, but I couldn't really hear what it was, because the kids on the other side of the line of cops were chanting louder, "WE HAVE TO GRADUATE, WE HAVE TO GRADUATE."

Their signs said, "Come Back to the Classroom," "Seniors Support Our Schools," and "We Need Our Diplomas."

As we approached the demonstrators, the kids on the teachers' side began to yell at us.

"Scabs! Scabs!" they shouted. "Don't go inside! Boycott! Go home!"

I began to feel like I definitely should have chosen today to stay home.

Then the kids on the other side began to scream at us.

"Why should you go to school if the teachers won't? No teachers, no students! Boycott! Go home! Stand up for your rights! Don't be a pawn in a power game!"

"Isn't that funny?" Iz shouted over the noise of the pickets. "They're on opposite sides but they both want us to do the same thing."

"That's good enough for me," Nat said. She turned and walked back across the street.

I looked nervously at Iz. "You going to go in?"

"Yeah."

"Why? What's the point?"

"Because I don't want to be intimidated by them."

"Yeah, well to tell you the truth, I'm kind of intimidated."

And here came Con and *her* group. I had to look two or three times at their signs and even then I didn't quite get the point.

"THE THIRD WORLD IS STARVING." "BOYCOTT GRAPES, LETTUCE AND TICO-TICO WINES." "MIGRANT WORKERS ARE LIVING IN POVERTY."

"You live like kings," Con shrieked at the teachers, "compared to the poor!"

Her group began to chant. "Feed the hungry, starve the rich, the president is a son-of-a-bitch!"

"Do you suppose," Iz grinned, "they mean the president of the school board, or the President of these here United States?"

"Whichever they mean, Iz, I'm even more intimidated than I was a minute ago."

"Come on, Julie, there's nothing to be afraid of. They have enough cops here to put down a small revolution."

"I think this may *be* a small revolution."

"Well, look, if you're really scared, why don't

you walk home with Nat? You sure won't miss anything. Except, possibly, a near riot." Her eyes lit up, as if she were actually looking forward to possible violence. Well, it *would* break the monotony.

"I'll stay," I decided suddenly. I really didn't like the idea of knuckling under to the mob either, although I had to wonder if sometimes it wasn't more sensible to knuckle under.

We walked between the two warring camps, with Con's group jeering right behind us.

"BOYCOTT! BOYCOTT!"

"GO HOME! SUPPORT OUR SCHOOLS! GO HOME! SUPPORT OUR SCHOOLS!"

"FEED THE HUNGRY, STARVE THE RICH, THE PRESIDENT IS A SON-OF-A-BITCH!"

"Wasn't that exciting?" Isobel said sarcastically as we sped toward the front entrance, having got past the worst of the demonstration.

"The high point of my day," I agreed breathlessly.

I hadn't even thought to look for Mr. Conrad.

Classes were barely half full. Some were consolidated, because a lot of the people who had been policing us before had failed to show up today, and it was soon apparent that the school was very short-handed.

At eleven o'clock, after I had witnessed two near fistfights in the halls, the principal took to the airwaves (the PA system) to restore calm.

And to give up.

"We've tried to keep the school open," he announced gravely, "so that we could keep the educational process ongoing."

Jeers and catcalls.

"What educational process?" someone behind me snickered.

"But I'm afraid that until further notice I'm going to have to ask you to stay home. The buses will be here in fifteen minutes. At that time there will be an orderly dismissal and you will all go *directly home*. No one will be allowed on school grounds after eleven-fifteen. The police will remain here to see that this order is enforced."

At eleven-fifteen, when we left, the picketing teachers were there *en masse*. Somehow, someone had managed to round up almost the entire striking staff, and they were milling around the street looking a lot more militant than they had in the previous six days.

Just as I came out of the building someone threw something toward the teachers. I didn't see what it was, but a roar went up among the students and about eight of the kids on the teachers' side charged the police lines to attack the Support Our Schools faction.

"FASCIST PIGS!" Suddenly the two groups of students were using their picket signs as weapons and all the kids coming out of the school began racing toward the mob to get a better view of the action. I was carried along with the crush, hoping I'd manage to stay in one piece and trying to keep up with the others so I wouldn't fall and get trampled to death. I wasn't all that scared, though. For some reason I felt more excitement than fear. Maybe it was because I was as eager to see what was going on as everyone else.

The small army of cops plunged into the middle of the sea of screamers, grabbing signs away from people and yanking students apart. There seemed to be more shouting and cursing than actual maiming and killing, but I certainly had to classify it as a Genuine Riot.

In a couple of minutes the principal came out and hustled all of us spectators around to the other side of the school toward freedom.

"Now go home!" he said. "All of you."

We had to walk around the block to get to where the buses were waiting, and as I got on my bus, I could see that the police were still wading through the mob trying to break it up.

The last thing I saw as the bus pulled away was Con Fabian, sitting on the shoulders of a husky companion and hitting someone over the head with the top half of her picket sign.

"Thank God," I gasped, when I finally got home and let myself in the front door. "I lived to tell the tale." That was, perhaps, overdramatizing it a bit. But after all, how many riots does the average person get to see in a lifetime?

There was a series of small rustling sounds from upstairs. I froze in the hallway and strained my ears. Mice? Mom? Muggers?

It couldn't be my mother, because her car

wasn't in the driveway. It was unlikely that mice would be able to make the audible footsteps I was now hearing, unless they were wearing very heavy boots. Just as I realized that by deductive reasoning that left only muggers, a male figure appeared at the top of the stairs.

"Julie!"

"Gabe!"

He ran downstairs and I threw my arms around him.

"What a shock! I didn't think you'd—"

Just then a female figure appeared at the top of the stairs. I let go of Gabe and stepped back, astonished.

"Gabe?" I asked hesitantly.

He turned around and saw the girl, who, it just then occurred to me, had been in Gabe's room with him when no one else was home.

I frowned.

"Come on down, Marlene," Gabe said. "This is the girl I wrote you about, remember?"

"I'd know her anywhere," I said coolly.

She was almost six feet tall and very thin. Her hair was a dirty blond and hung rather limply around her face. She wore faded, slightly ragged jeans and a yellow T-shirt with the letters "SWPP" stenciled on it. She vaguely reminded me of someone.

She trudged down the steps almost as if she were reluctant to join us.

She had very bad posture.

"Marlene, this is my little sister, Julie. Julie, Marlene Slack."

"How's it going?" she asked indifferently.

"As well as can be expected," I replied with a shrug.

Gabe looked from Marlene to me speculatively.

"Well," he said. "Well. I thought I'd surprise you all. Won't the folks be surprised, Julie?"

"Oh, you bet," I agreed. "They certainly will be surprised."

Who *did* she remind me of?

"Well," Gabe repeated.

"Why don't we," I suggested finally, "all go into the kitchen and have a nice cup of tea."

"Great idea!" Gabe enthused. "Great. A nice cup of tea would really hit the spot right now. Let's go make some tea."

It seemed to me that Gabe was a little more hysterical about the idea of tea than was normal, but Marlene managed to stay quite composed.

I led them into the kitchen.

I made the tea and set out some cookies I managed to dredge up from the breadbox.

We sat down at the table.

"Milk?" I asked Marlene, gesturing toward the container. "Sugar?"

"No thanks," she said. She pulled a little silver flask out of her hip pocket, unscrewed the cap and sloshed a shot of whatever was in it into her cup. Then she offered the flask to Gabe.

I scowled. Gabe looked at me, then shook his head.

"Ah, no thanks, Marl."

Marl shrugged, capped the flask and stuck it back into her pocket.

"Are you allowed to drink when you're in training?" I asked innocently.

"In training for what?"

"Oh, Gabe told us you were really into track, running and stuff."

"Not like on a team thing!" Marlene said, as if she were genuinely shocked that I could suggest such a thing. "Not *organized* sports; *God*, no." Her face plainly expressed her feelings about organized sports; in Marlene's hierarchy of evil, they obviously ranked somewhere between child abuse and strip mining.

"Then you just run for the sheer love of running?" I concluded.

"I guess you could put it that way."

"So what's new at home?" Gabe asked.

"The teachers are on strike. They've been trying to keep the schools open, but they sent us home early today and told us to stay home until further notice. And there was practically a riot in front of the school when we got out."

"A riot?" You could almost see Marlene's ears prick up. It was the first spark of interest she'd shown since she'd met me.

"Yeah. People screaming and fighting and cops and everything."

"Oh, Gabe," she breathed, "let's go look." Her eyes shone.

"You want to?" asked Gabe.

"Oh, yes. Do you think," she asked, turning to me with a look of expectant hope, "they'll still be rioting?"

"Gee, I don't know. The cops were trying to break it up when I left."

She jumped up from her chair. "Come on, Gabe, let's go over there."

"Okay. You want to come, Jule?"

"No thanks," I said. "I've seen my quota of riots for today."

"Oh, I hope they're still there," Marlene was saying animatedly as they left the house.

I sat glumly over the rest of my tea and pondered. Gradually the image of Marlene's face melted away and in its place another set of features formed. Of *course*. *That's* who she reminded me of.

"Gabe! What a surprise!"

My mother hugged and kissed him, then stood back to look at him.

"Didn't you see the car out front?" he asked.

"Yes, but I didn't even guess it might be you. I thought it was one of Julie's friends."

My father came in the back way from the garage.

"There's a strange girl in the kitchen—" he started to say, then saw Gabe.

"Hey!" he yelled, and threw his arms around him. "Hey, when did you get in?"

"This afternoon. Thought I'd surprise you."

"Who's in the kitchen?" asked my mother.

"And is she all right?" my father asked. "She looks kind of depressed."

"Oh, she's just disappointed we missed the riot. Marlene! Hey, Marlene, come meet my folks."

"What riot?" demanded my mother. "Gabe, are they rioting up there?"

"Not up there," I corrected. "Down here."

Marlene sauntered into the hallway where we were all still clustered.

"This is Marlene Slack, the girl I wrote you about. Marlene, my parents."

"How's it going?" Marlene said automatically.

"Hello, Marlene," my mother said. "We're glad to have you. *What riot down here?*" she demanded, turning to me.

"At school. The pickets got a little out of hand."

"Nine people injured," Marlene said dolefully. "And we missed the whole thing."

"Well, thank goodness for that," my mother said. Marlene shook her head in disgust, as if she would never understand people like my mother. I think my mother's long look at Marlene probably meant the same thing.

"Are you all right, Julie?" my father finally asked.

"Oh, sure, I wasn't even anywhere near it. But they told us to stay home until further notice."

"What are we all standing here for?" my father said suddenly. "Let's go sit down and get acquainted."

"I want to get dinner started," my mother said. "Why don't you all come into the kitchen and keep me company?"

My mother began to amass ingredients for her fifteen-minute chili while my father made the salad and I set the table.

"Gabe tells us you're a track enthusiast," my father commented.

"I'm not on the team or anything," she said. "I just run . . . for the love of running."

My head jerked up. I peered over at Gabe to see if he'd noticed that Marlene had used practically my exact words. His eyes were fixed on her face, and he wore a silly little grin. Even if the phrase had sounded familiar to him, he probably thought that Marlene originated it.

Well, I thought sourly, at least she recognizes a good line when she hears one.

"That's . . . admirable," my father said.

"Yeah. Well." Marlene shrugged.

"What are you majoring in, Marlene?" my mother asked.

"Sociology."

"She's really into urban studies, group activism, local control, like that," Gabe said proudly.

"And penology and prison conditions," Marlene added.

"Oh, you're into jail, too," I remarked brightly.

My mother frowned at me, but Marlene didn't react at all.

"Where's your home?" my father asked.

"Grosse Pointe. Michigan."

"Well, you're a long way from home," my mother said.

Marlene shrugged.

The chili was ready. We sat down at the kitchen table.

"I made plenty of salad," my father said. "In case you don't eat chili, Marlene."

"Why shouldn't I eat chili?"

"I thought—well—" my father seemed a little flustered. "In case you were a vegetarian or something."

Gabe grinned broadly. "Watch out for those snap judgments, Dad," he said wickedly.

My father took a consuming interest in his chili.

When coffee was served Marlene started to reach into her pocket. I waited eagerly for her to pull out the little flask, but at that moment she happened to look up and catch Gabe's eye. He frowned, ever so slightly and gave a barely perceptible shake of his head.

Marlene didn't even seem to react, but her hand came up from her pocket empty.

I leaned back in my chair, faintly disappointed.

After we finished eating, Gabe and Marlene went to visit a friend of his who was attending a local college. My parents seemed to relax the moment they were out the door.

"Well," my mother said helplessly.

My father cleared his throat. "An interesting girl."

"Interesting?" I repeated. "She's not exactly what you'd call a stimulating conversationalist."

"She's probably very . . . deep," he said.

I thought Marlene was about as deep as a puddle after a five minute drizzle, but perhaps what he meant was that whatever good qualities she might have were hidden way beneath that surly surface.

"It's funny," my mother mused. "She's *just* the way I pictured her. I thought maybe—well, you know how Gabe's letters are . . ."

"He exaggerates so much," my father said weakly.

"Yes," she agreed. "So I'd sort of hoped . . ."

"Look at it this way," my father said, trying to sound optimistic. "If Marlene turned out to be just the way he described her, let's be grateful he didn't bring Carlos home to visit."

On Saturday Gabe announced that they had changed their plans. Instead of returning to school on Sunday afternoon they thought they might stay until Monday night. Marlene, it seems, really had her heart set on visiting the scene of the riot, in the hopes that there would be a rerun of Friday's violence.

"But what about your classes?" my mother asked.

"Oh, don't worry about that; I've got plenty of cuts left. One more day won't matter."

"But the principal told everyone to stay home,"

my mother went on, looking more worried by the minute.

"But the constitution guarantees freedom of assembly," Marlene pointed out. "And those who are truly dedicated to their cause should exercise their constitutional right to demonstrate no matter what the principal says."

"It's not the principal," I suggested. "It's the principle of the thing."

"Exactly," said Marlene, without cracking a smile. (I don't know why I kept hoping that she might have a sense of humor.)

"Marlene feels she ought to be there to help the cause," Gabe explained.

"What cause?" asked my mother.

"I want to take my stand," Marlene said, "with those who are fighting for freedom and justice."

"Which ones are those?" I asked.

She looked at me blankly.

"Which side are you going to take your stand with?"

"The side that's for freedom and justice," she said, as if the answer should have been obvious to a slow three-year-old.

"But how do you—"

I was about to ask how Marlene knew which side was for freedom and justice when my father snapped on the radio to "get some news" and effectively stifled me.

". . . and Harold Miller, president of the Glenhollow Teachers' Association, is urging his members to return to school on Monday. Miller said that in view of the progress made in negotiations and the unfortunate violence which occurred Friday, during which four people were slightly injured and eight arrests were made, he felt the responsible course of action was to return to the classrooms while the settlement is being ironed out."

"Well, that ends your vacation, Julie," my father said, almost as if he expected me to be disappointed.

"I guess so," I agreed, trying not to leap up and dance around the living room.

I could see Mr. Conrad on Monday. He would read that composition I'd written just before the strike. He would ask me to stay after school to discuss it. He would recognize a kindred spirit. We would—

"Just my luck," Marlene muttered sourly.

"Con Fabian to the core," I remarked.

Whoops.

I leaned back on the couch, feeling foolish, as everybody turned to look at me.

"I was just thinking of someone Marlene reminded me of," I said lamely.

"Con Fabian?" my father asked.

"You know—the assistant editor of *Taproots*."

"Oh," he said, not yet remembering. Then, "*Oh*."

"Oh dear," my mother said faintly. But I don't think Marlene heard her.

134

9. TEACHERS MAY IMPOSE DETENTION ON ANY STUDENT WHOSE BEHAVIOR OR ACADEMIC PERFORMANCE IS MARKEDLY DEFICIENT. DETENTION WILL BE SERVED AFTER DISMISSAL IN THE HOMEROOM OF THE TEACHER WHO IMPOSES IT.

Mr. Conrad was new to AGGMHS, and I realized that I was probably not the only girl in school who thought he made your average Adonis look tacky.

After all, I had the example of Natalie, who sat right next to me in English and who, as I've said, is a nonstop talker. Before the bell rang, and before Mr. Conrad entered the room, Nat would keep up a constant stream of chatter about the events of the day. She always had a number of things to tell me, things that had happened since we'd talked on the phone the night before and she began her monologue the moment I slid into the seat next to her.

However, as soon as Mr. Conrad walked into the room Nat's mouth froze in midsentence. She would slowly, carefully clasp her hands in her lap, fix her eyes on Mr. Conrad's face, and lapse into utter silence for the next forty-two minutes.

When the bell rang signaling the end of the period, Nat would sigh heavily, pile her books together with great effort and murmur, "Isn't he *incredible?*"

The first time she said this I managed to reply in a whisper, "He is such stuff as dreams are made of," but after a couple of days I stopped answering; by that time I was doing a lot of heavy sighing myself.

At first it seemed enough just to be one of the privileged few to sit in his presence once a day. Gazing at his face, watching his movements around the room, listening to him describe the elements of a short story nourished those of us who hungered for beauty in our everyday lives.

Then, for a few days, I was almost able to convince myself that he said my name in a special way when he called the roll. The little pause after he said, "Howe," as if he were clinging to the memory of my name and reluctant to let it go and just zip on to the next one . . . the hesitation, the uncertainty in his voice, as if just the thought of me had so moved him he found it hard to continue . . .

It must have been wishful thinking on my part, or else I was so blinded and deafened by love that it took me a good week before I finally realized that the boy after me on the class list, Charles Hrynyshyn, might very well have disconcerted Mr. Conrad more than I.

The *Graebner Gab,* our school paper, ran a little picture of Mr. Conrad under the heading, "New Faces at AGGMHS." I hadn't even opened the paper when Nat pointed it out to me before English class.

"You mean you didn't *see* it yet?" She ripped open her copy and pointed to the photo.

"It's a little blurry," she admitted, "but still, don't you think his smile really—"

Mr. Conrad had just entered the room. Nat folded up the paper without taking her eyes off him and carefully slid it into the desk.

As soon as class was over I opened my paper and rapidly read the little profile they had of him under the picture.

"Likes opera, basketball and skiing. Admits to being addicted to chocolate chip cookies. Currently at work on a novel . . ."

A novel! Mr. Conrad was a writer! What an incredible coincidence, I thought, speeding through the hall to my next class.

"Julie, I had no idea. Under my very eyes, a talent like yours . . . and a novel, at your age. I'm really honored that you asked me to read it. Of course, it's not perfect; there are some rough spots. I thought maybe we could go over it together if you wouldn't resent a few suggestions? Maybe, tonight? . . ."

But when I got home that afternoon the dream seemed a bit farfetched. By the time I had a novel written I'd probably be graduating, and I just couldn't wait that long for Mr. Conrad to realize he loved me.

Now, chocolate chip cookies on the other hand . . .

I sat down in English class, my little paper bag of chocolate chip cookies stuck inside my big canvas purse. On the desk in front of the room were eight boxes, in various wrappings, of various sizes. Natalie was sheepishly returning to her seat after dropping her box next to the others, when Mr. Conrad walked into the room.

He was carrying four boxes of various sizes, with various wrappings, and two brown paper bags.

When he saw the packages on his desk he seemed to almost recoil. His step faltered for a moment, his beautiful eyes appeared to glaze over and it looked as if he might have some difficulty reaching the desk.

"Well, well," he said weakly. He made a noble attempt at a cheerful smile. "Are all these for me?"

I had put my father's recording of *Il Trovatore* on the stereo and was nearly dozing off on the couch out of sheer boredom, when my father came home.

"Is it possible," he asked my mother incredulously, "that she is actually *sleeping* through the Anvil Chorus?"

"Anything's possible," my mother replied, raising her voice to be heard over the clanging.

"I'm not sleeping," I said, my eyes still shut. "I'm extremely interested."

"You could have fooled me," he said. "When did you become extremely interested in opera?"

"When I decided that I was a musical illiterate," I replied, "and realized I needed a good dose of culture."

"And are you getting a good dose of culture?"

"I think I've overdosed," I admitted sourly, and hauled myself off the couch and out of the room.

I'd never make it as an opera buff, that was perfectly clear. Skiing, of course, was out of the question, but that didn't matter. We still had the love of literature and writing to help strengthen the bond between us—once there was a bond to strengthen—and that certainly would be enough. Any time now, he'd begin to notice the really outstanding quality of my themes and the spark of a budding writer whom he'd want to encourage and—

After weeks of straight "A" work in English Mr. Conrad still showed no particular interest in my potential.

He did not request a private conference with me after school.

"Julie, you're so far beyond what my other students are capable of. Your insights are so—so *profound,* so much more wise than I'd expect from a sophomore. You're not like the others . . . you're . . . I know I shouldn't be saying this—"

And he didn't.

After a certain amount of time, the experience of unrequited passion is resolved in one of two ways: either it pales and fades away from lack of encouragement and the conclusion that the thing is hopeless, or you finally determine to do something to set off a spark of response in the person you love.

I reached that fork-in-the-road shortly after the strike, when my beautiful composition, on which I had worked so hard and on which I had practically pinned my last hopes, was returned by Mr. Conrad without a word, and with only the usual red ink "A. Good work." on the top.

I was sick with disappointment. The rest of the period passed by nearly unnoticed. I don't even remember if I looked up at his face once, so preoccupied was I with fighting to keep back tears.

He didn't know I was alive. I was no more important to him than any other student he had. I was as insignificant as a mosquito on the Taj Mahal and he was going to continue to ignore me for the rest of the year.

I couldn't bear the thought of that. For him never to know, never to recognize how I felt; that someone who had such force, such impact on my life should go blithely on through his own, without ever feeling *my* influence on him, was simply unthinkable.

Yet he steadfastly and stubbornly refused to notice me.

As long as I continued to respond when called

on, to hand in my work on time, to excel in his class and not to require any of his concern or attention, he wouldn't *give* me any of that concern or attention. Why should he? I was no trouble.

And that was when I conceived my brilliant idea.

As day is to night; as Dr. Jekyll is to Mr. Hyde; as good is to evil; so did the New Julie contrast with the Old Julie.

I started simply.

When Mr. Conrad called on me in class I couldn't answer his questions.

"Didn't you read the assignment?" he asked, surprised that the person who was first with her hand up on any given question was now gazing at him stupidly.

I shook my head and cast my eyes downward.

"Well there's not much use in coming to class if you don't bother preparing for it."

Now, that was more than he'd ever said to me before in class. Usually he'd say, "That's right," or "Very good," and go right on. This was *progress*.

I began to neglect handing in my homework.

I nearly flunked two tests. (I was very careful about that. I didn't want to screw things up so completely that once I'd managed to interest Mr. Conrad I'd find my entire semester's average destroyed.)

Eventually I knew he'd have to do something.

He couldn't let me go on like this without taking some punitive steps to at least force me to do the homework.

And at last . . .

It was the fourth theme I didn't do and when he handed back everyone else's he said, "You didn't do this assignment either?"

He looked almost angry. My stomach jumped and I swallowed hard. It was glorious to have him look at me that way, finally, with some emotion on his face, some reaction to me other than complete indifference.

"Look, you're going to have to start making some of these things up. I want you down here at three for detention or the next four days and I expect you to make up a theme each day until you're caught up."

My heart pounded crazily. It was all happening the way it was supposed to. This afternoon when I came down, he'd asked me why I had suddenly fallen off in my work. Was anything wrong? Was there, maybe, some difficulty at home?

"Well, to tell you the truth, Mr. Conrad, things are a little rough for me right now—emotionally, I mean. Sometimes I wonder . . . is any of this *worth* it? Life can be so—so very *lousy*."

He would be filled with concern. At first that's all it would be, just concern. He would talk to me, reason with me, try to be supportive and kind and convince me that a young, beautiful girl like me had everything to live for.

Then, later, much later, say after a couple of

months, I'd confess my little deception and he'd roar with laughter, then clasp me to him and murmur, "What a precious little liar you are . . ."

I functioned zombielike through my last class, which was typing. God only knows what I typed when we were supposed to be doing our exercises. (Mrs. Ross gently asked me the next day to do the lesson over when I had a spare fifteen minutes, but never did give me back whatever it was I handed in.)

At three o'clock, my weak legs barely carried me to Mr. Conrad's room.

He glanced up as I walked in. He pointed toward a desk and said, "Start with the assignment on Walter Mitty. Do you remember what you were supposed to do?"

I did, of course. I remembered everything he ever said, but I shook my head anyway, just so he would have to talk to me a little more.

"Write a personality profile of Walter Mitty or his wife."

That was all he said. And it was the last time he looked up at me until I dropped the paper on his desk and left, seething with rage.

I'd waited for him to start questioning me and he never opened his mouth.

I had to walk a mile home and began to calm down as I neared my house. It was probably just that he was too busy to talk to me this afternoon. All those papers to mark, things on his mind.

Tomorrow afternoon he'd probably have nothing to occupy him and he would begin to show his real concern for me.

But the following day, when I got to Mr. Conrad's room, there were two other students there. They were just sitting down at desks and beginning to work on something, and I knew with despair that he could never talk to me with *them* in the room.

Bitterly disappointed, I flung myself into a chair, yanked open my looseleaf, and began to write the second composition I owed him, without even pretending that I didn't know what the assignment was.

On the third day of my detentions, I found Mr. Conrad's room empty of other students. Mr. Conrad was reading *The New York Times*.

I sat down at the desk I'd sat at before and made a pretense of beginning to write. I was so close to him—hardly ten feet away. Every time the newspaper rustled, every time he turned a page, my heart jumped. *When would he put down that damn paper and start talking to me?*

The room phone rang shrilly and I was so tense I nearly leaped out of my seat.

Mr. Conrad went to answer it. I kept my eyes glued to my paper.

"Oh, hi, Liz. Sure, pretty soon."

Liz? I didn't even try to keep up the pretense of writing. I sat stock still, frozen in my position, and hung on every word.

"Sure, okay. Should I write it down? All right, what? Right. Right, I got it. Pampers, the overnight ones, and the junior beef dinner. What? Still cranky? Must be the teething. Okay, hon. See you later."

He hung up the phone.

I exhaled, slowly, silently. I was going to keep a very firm grip on myself.

Pampers are diapers. Diapers are for babies. Teething is what babies do. Junior beef dinners are what babies eat. Liz is a woman's name. Unless he was talking to his sister about a toothless, unhousebroken dog which they treated like an infant, Mr. Conrad was married and had a kid.

I felt empty.

All these months I'd been carrying around a nice little bundle of love in my heart, ready to give it to Mr. Conrad when the right moment presented itself. Suddenly he was no longer the virile young novelist who skied on weekends and grew passionate to the strains of fiery sopranos; now he was the suburban father who schlepped Pampers home from the supermarket and burped a baby over his shoulder.

His beautiful, beautiful shoulder.

I looked up at him. He was again engrossed in *The New York Times*. He still looked like Robert Redford, without the wart on his cheek.

I still had to regulate my breathing as I looked at him.

Why hadn't the *Graebner Gab* mentioned that he was married? Why would they bother with dumb, insignificant things like chocolate chip cookies and novel-writing, and go and leave out the kind of vital information that can make or break a budding relationship?

If he'd been married twenty years, if his children were grown and his wife a drunk or a nag, maybe I could still hold onto some shred of hope that he would be receptive, even eager for the kind of young love I could offer.

But he was married and he was fairly young himself, and it was not likely that he'd married a wealthy fifty-year-old woman—and there was a *baby,* for heaven's sake.

I hope he drools on your manuscript, I thought darkly.

I hope he teethes on your skis.

I hope he burps all over your beautiful burgundy turtleneck.

That didn't make me feel a whole lot better, but it helped.

Barely concentrating on what I was writing, I dashed off the stupid theme I was supposed to be doing and then, without stopping, scrawled the fourth one that I would have done the following afternoon.

There was really no point in dragging this farce out any longer.

I dropped the two themes on his desk, gathered up my books, straightened my shoulders and walked out of Mr. Conrad's life.

I didn't cry at all until I got home.

10. THERE WILL BE NO SELL-ING OF ANY ITEMS ON SCHOOL GROUNDS EXCEPT FOR THOSE ARTICLES SOLD AT THE STUDENT STORE.

The Student Store operated out of a converted classroom in the business and commercial training section of the school. It was run by business students and stocked everything from plush puppies in the contrasting Graebner colors of royal blue and white, to looseleaf binders.

At least, they *claimed* they stocked all those things.

This particular morning, I had hurried in before homeroom to pick up two perfectly simple items.

"I need a refill for a Jotter," I said, "and a package of looseleaf paper."

The girl behind the makeshift counter rummaged through her pitifully inadequate supply of writing implements.

"We're out of Jotter refills. What color looseleaf paper do you want?"

"I think white is kind of classic."

"Lots of people think the colored paper is fun," she said brightly. "We have pink and yellow."

"I don't suppose it comes scented," I mumbled.

"No, but that's an idea, isn't it?"

Not much of one, I thought sourly. Tinted looseleaf paper was not my idea of fun, but since I was entirely without anything to write on for the day (and would probably be without anything to write *with* too) I settled on the pink.

"Do you have any Skrip cartridges?" I had a battered cartridge pen somewhere in the bottom of my bag and I could always use that in a pinch.

"Oh, yes," she trilled, "we have those. Would you like turquoise blue or permanent red?"

"How about just plain blue or just plain black?"

She shook her head. "We're out of those."

Cursing myself for not planning ahead, for continuing to fall for the propaganda that you could get anything you needed at the Student Store, I paid her for the looseleaf paper but turned down the cartridges. I just couldn't see writing with permanent red ink on pink paper, or with turquoise blue ink on pink paper either. People might begin to think I was affected, or worse, a frivolous, bubbleheaded type.

To be honest, I had been through the colored looseleaf paper phase in the ninth grade, but I had outgrown it after my first flirtation with "fun" paper. It cost a lot more than the white paper and since half the girls in the class were also using it, it lost any impact it might have had on my teachers.

"Why don't you take a nice Bic just to get you through the day?" the girl suggested.

"Yeah, maybe I'd better." I fumbled through my wallet to take out the change I'd just put in there.

"Julie, my flower, my budding blossom of womanhood!"

I turned around to find Damion Flamm hovering at my left elbow.

"Damion, my apprentice con man."

"Damion Flamm, you get out of here," the girl behind the counter ordered. "It's bad enough to have you standing right outside our door stealing our customers—"

"I have," he said out of the corner of his mouth, "Skrip cartridges and Jotter refills. Care to step outside?"

Mr. Hoover, the chairman of the business department, strode toward Damion.

"Scram, Flamm." He gestured toward the door with his thumb.

" 'Scram, Flamm,' " Damion repeated. "That's very good. I was just leaving, Mr. H."

"Do you want the Bic?" the girl asked me.

"Uh, no thanks. I can probably borrow a pen."

I followed Damion outside the room. We stood a little down the hall from the Student Store and he reached into his bulging trenchcoat pockets and dug out a Jotter refill and a package of permanent black Skrip cartridges.

149

"How much?"

"For you," he said grandly, "a dollar."

I looked at him suspiciously.

"That's pretty cheap, Damion. Are you sure they aren't stolen or something?"

"Hot pen refills?" he howled. "You've got to be kidding. No, my innocent little primrose, there is no profit in stealing stocks of Jotter refills."

"Well how can you sell them so cheap?"

"I know a guy," he said vaguely.

I handed him a dollar.

"Now my watches," he began confidentially. He raised his eyebrows and lowered his voice. "My watches, on the other hand . . ."

He let the last sentence hang there, unfinished, allowing the suspicions of shady dealings in stolen goods take root in my mind.

"The watches are hot," I concluded.

"I didn't say that," he went on hastily. "Now, I never said that."

I shook my head. "Damion, you're impossible. You *want* people to think your stuff is stolen, so they think they'll be getting a terrific deal on it."

Damion tried to look as innocent as he could, which, for Damion, was not easy.

"Listen, I've got to run. I'm glad you had the stuff I needed."

"Anytime, sweetness. Anytime."

My relationship with Damion Flamm had, up to then, been strictly business. It was merely a matter of supply and demand. He supplied what

I—and a lot of other kids—demanded. Damion regarded himself as a public service, and there was an element of truth to that. He sold things that the Student Store always seemed to be out of and he sold them cheaper than you could get them at a regular store. And he was there when you needed him.

"Julie, my little persimmon—"

"Damion, my potential swindler of widows and orphans, if you ever call me your little watermelon it's all over between us."

"That would devastate me," he declared, holding one hand solemnly over his heart as if the Pledge of Allegiance were being spoken. "I'd also be devastated," he added in a businesslike tone, "if you went in *there* to buy instead of seeing me first." He tilted his head toward the Student Store.

"I wouldn't dream of it. I only came here because I knew I'd find *you*. I need some looseleaf reinforcements."

"Julie, there comes a time in every man's life—"

"Listen, Damion, if this is a marriage proposal I ought to tell you that my mother promised me to an Indian prince when I was six."

"It's not a proposal. It's more like a proposition."

"Oh?"

"A *business* proposition."

"For heaven's sake, Damion, what kind of a deal can we make on a twenty-nine cent package of reinforcements?"

"For you, fifteen," he said automatically. "But that's not what I meant."

"Fifteen cents? Damion, how do you *do* it?"

"Will you please listen a minute?" he said irritably.

"I'm sorry, it's just that I'm kind of in a hurry and am afraid I'll be late for homeroom."

"So they'll start the PA announcements without you," he said, exasperated.

"All right, I'm listening."

He looked so odd standing there in the middle of the hall, with his shabby tan raincoat, pockets bulging with all sorts of merchandise. No one but Damion wore a trenchcoat like that; even with his back to you, from twenty feet away, without being able to see the fire of the supersalesman in his eyes, without being able to see either the black-framed glasses he wore or the faded flannel shirts, you would recognize Damion.

"What I started to say was, there comes a time in every *businessman's* life when he discovers he needs extra help. Now, when I discovered that I could use a partner I thought to myself, Damion, you've got a gold mine here. You have a thriving business, you have a solid reputation for rock-bottom prices, you've built up goodwill among your customers, and now it's time to expand. The territory is too big, too potentially rich for one man to handle."

It was all I could do to keep from tapping my foot and glancing impatiently at my watch. I *had* to get down to my homeroom and Damion chose *now* to deliver a lecture on Business Success.

"But with expansion," Damion droned on relentlessly, "comes risk. Your partner, who would be working on his own at the other end of the building, might overcharge the customers. Or he might hold out some of the take for himself. In other words, if you pick the wrong person he could cheat you, or cheat the public. Then, whoosh, all the things you've struggled to build up over the years" (Damion was a sophomore) "are gone, just like *that*." His face looked grave, as if the unspeakable had already happened.

"Do you see what I mean?"

"I do," I said fervently. "I really do." Not for the world would I have run the risk of telling him I didn't quite understand, and have him start all over again from the beginning.

The first bell rang.

"Damion, I—"

He raised his hand. "One more minute. There's still the late bell."

The late bell rings three minutes after the first bell, and since I have to go way over to the west end of the building and down two flights of stairs to get from the Student Store to my homeroom, his unconcern was less than reassuring.

"So I said to myself, Damion, who is the one person in the whole school who you would not only trust with your aging grandmother, but who you would like to see profit from this business association? Who, in this whole school, do you really want to give a piece of the action to? And who," he said, showing all his teeth and nearly blinding me, "do you think I came up with?"

"I—I can't imagine," I said faintly. We both knew I could very well imagine who he meant.

"You, my little larkspur. None other than you."

"Damion—I—this is so sudden." What was I to say? I didn't have the least little yearning to be Damion's assistant, I didn't feel at all as if I could possibly be a super-duper salesperson, and I just couldn't see myself standing in the halls in an ancient trenchcoat stuffed with pencils, erasers and ring binders, buttonholing the passing throngs and urging them to sample my wares.

The late bell rang.

"Damion, I really have to *run*."

And I ran. But not before Damion could shout after me, "I'll meet you after school and we'll work everything out!"

Damion was waiting for me right by the front steps at three o'clock. Nat and Isobel rolled their eyes at each other as he grabbed my arm.

"Damion, I'll miss my bus!" I wailed.

"So I'll walk you home. It's not that far."

"It's a mile and a half, almost! You don't even know where I live."

"Okay, okay, I'll take your bus and we'll talk at your house and then *I'll* walk the mile and a half."

He followed me to the bus. Nat and Izzie got on before me and took a seat together, leaving me to sit next to Damion. I shot them a hostile look. Nat giggled. Isobel's eyes twinkled. She looked out the window and began to hum.

"Now, here's how we'll work it," Damion began.

He was still talking when we got off at my stop. He trailed me to the house and didn't even wait to be asked in.

He had it all worked out.

I would sell half the stock and make one-fourth of the profits. He would give me the stuff every morning and we'd settle up every afternoon. All I had to do was stand near the Student Store with him for a few days, till everyone got to know me and to know that they could come to me for all the things they needed and then he'd station himself at the west end of the building on the second floor and work there.

I got Cokes from the refrigerator and sat down wearily at the kitchen table. He took a chair opposite me and went on.

"I tell you, it's a gold mine, Julie, a gold mine."

"There's gold in them there refills," I said, my heart not really in it.

"That's good," he crowed, "that's very good. And it's true, too."

"No, Damion."

"It's not good?" he asked, a little confused.

"No, it's not particularly good, but what I'm really saying is no, I don't want to be a salesman."

"Julie, my flowering quince, you'd make a wonderful salesperson. Your face just glows with honest innocence. You'd inspire confidence in everyone, you're polite, smart, hard-working—"

"Thrifty, reverent and morally straight," I finished for him. "Damion, my budding bunco artist, I am no salesman. I have no talent in that field. If I started to sell gravestones people would stop dying."

"Cute," said Damion. "Not original, but cute."

"See? I steal jokes. I'm not a paragon of virtue."

"I should hope not," he shuddered. "You don't want to overdo that virtue bit. Did you say morally straight?"

"Yes, I did."

"Too bad." He leered. Damion does a lousy leer. He looked about as much a threat to my morals as Captain Kangaroo.

"Listen to me," he said. "You don't know what you're turning down. Let me give it to you in dollars and cents. You know what I make a day, working alone in that one little spot? Guess."

"I have no idea. I can't even make a guess."

"I net about five dollars a day. Sometimes more, sometimes less. Now with you and me both working, that ought to be ten dollars, right?"

"I suppose so."

"What's one-fourth of ten dollars?" he asked.

"Four into ten goes two," I mused.

"Two-fifty," he said helpfully. "That's twelve-fifty a *week*. Where else are you going to make that kind of money?"

"Are you kidding? As a migrant worker for one thing. Or a—"

"But, Julie, I'm talking about like fifteen minutes a *day*. That's about *twelve dollars an hour*. And if we sell a watch . . ." He spread out his hands, palms upward, as if to indicate the sky was the limit in this business.

"Oh, Damion, how often do you sell a watch?"

"How often do you *have* to sell one?" he retorted. "Sell just one and we could practically take the rest of the week off."

"No, Damion."

"Julie, do you mean to tell me you have everything that money can buy? That there isn't *something* you want so badly that you can taste it, but can't scratch up the bread to buy it?"

I hesitated. That's the kind of a question that people who make pacts with the devil get asked.

As it happened, there was this incredible suede jacket I had seen in a store about a week before. I'd tried it on and it looked magnificent on me, but it was eighty dollars. My mother had said she'd go halves with me, but she wasn't spending any eighty dollars on a jacket when I had two perfectly good jackets already, one of which was practically brand new and had cost her *plenty*.

This struck me as harsh but logical; it didn't, however, quash my desire to have the jacket, nor stop me from remembering the gorgeous reflection of myself in the store mirror. I had twenty dollars that I'd saved. By the time I saved up the rest it would be spring, and the jacket probably wouldn't even be in stock any more, and if it was, there wouldn't be much of a season left to wear it in.

However. On the other hand.

If I worked for Damion for a mere two weeks, I would be able to get the jacket almost immediately. Maybe even immediately if I told my mother I was working and she just had to advance me the twenty dollars I was short; not even advance it, because I could put the jacket on her charge account and by the time the bill came in I'd have the whole forty dollars.

As I say, I hesitated. And Damion, supersalesman that he was, saw that I was weakening.

He smiled broadly, dazzling me again with all those teeth.

"There *is* something, isn't there?" His voice was low and coaxing. I imagine the serpent talked that way to Eve when they discussed apples.

"Well . . ."

Thus, with grave doubts and a certain amount of out-and-out greed, did I become Damion's business partner.

"Damion, where *do* you get all this stuff?"

"Ah, Julie, my phlox, why worry yourself about that? Isn't that why I get three quarters and you get one quarter? Because I have all the aggravation of dealing with suppliers? All you have to do is take the suckers' money and hand 'em their pencils."

"But, Damion, if there's any question about

this stuff—I mean, if there's any possibility that we're doing something *illegal*—"

"You cut me to the quick! Do you think I'd get a sweet, innocent child like you mixed up in anything even *slightly* shady? Even *remotely* tainted with the tinge of something sordid?"

I noticed he had not answered my question. But I have to admit I didn't press him any further.

For two days I stood with Damion near the Student Store. Damion wore a little mechanical coin dispenser on his belt and offered to get me one, but I refused. I thought it looked sort of over-commercial and I reminded myself I was only in this for two weeks, and on a casual kind of basis. (Although I had not mentioned this time limit to Damion.) And mechanical coin changers attached to your belt were tacky.

The third day he left me there on my own.

"You are ready," he announced. "I am pushing the fledgling out of the nest. *Fly!*" He patted my cheek and raced down the hall toward the stairs.

I stood there, alone, my shopping bag full of school supplies at my feet and, to be perfectly honest, I tried to melt in with the rest of the students. I couldn't bring myself to stop people going into the store and whisper, out of the side of my mouth, "Psst. Make you a deal on erasers." I just couldn't do it.

The only sales I made were to a couple of kids who recognized me as Damion's partner and approached *me*. And I sold a Bic pen to Natalie and two pencils to Isobel.

"Do you think," Isobel asked drily, "your future lies in sales?"

"Oh, shut up, Isobel," I growled.

"Two dollars?" Damion said incredulously. "You only made *two dollars?*"

"Listen, Damion, I told you I wasn't very good at this. And I was right. Maybe we'd better forget the whole thing."

"Nonsense! *Nonsense!* You're just new at the game. Underneath that shy little peach blossom beats the heart of a tiger lily."

"Even for *you* that doesn't make sense," I muttered.

"You just have to be a little more assertive, a little more confident. You're doing *them* a favor you know, providing *them* with a service that they can't get anyplace else. You have to *believe* in your product and believe in *yourself* and you'll convey that belief to everyone else."

"I don't know . . ."

"You'll see. You'll do fine."

The next day, however, Damion's words were nearly forgotten. For five minutes all I could do was stand there as I had done the day before, and wait for people to come to me. When nobody did, I suddenly took myself in hand.

Look, I told myself, you're standing here and suffering because you want that jacket. At this rate it's going to take six weeks before you earn twenty dollars. That's six weeks of long, slow suffering, instead of two weeks of short, acute suffering. If you just *make an effort* for two weeks, this will all be over and you'll have your jacket.

I reminded myself of how I managed to imitate a female jock (a jockette? a jockess?) for those weeks in gym; if I could act like an athlete, I told myself, I could act like *anything*.

I gave myself the kind of pep talk that coaches usually save for the half-times of championship games.

And in the twinkling of an eye, I was Julie Howe, Big Time Operator. Salesperson *extraordinaire*. Go-getter.

"You say you need an Artgum eraser? Tell you what I'm gonna do . . ."

"Why pay more at the Student Store? Here's Howe, to sell you the best for less."

I actually stopped people outside the Store and said, "I can give it to you wholesale. You know they never have what you want in there. Try me first because you'll end up back here anyway. Save yourself some time and save money."

On and on I spieled, sounding almost like the barker at a carnival sideshow. No matter how idiotic I felt I kept at it, and in twenty minutes I had made seven dollars.

That afternoon, when I showed Damion the money, he was exultant.

"See, I knew you could do it! A born salesman!"

Friday evening, Damion came over to divide the profits and give me my share of the week's take. I wasn't entitled to too much, because I had really only made about twelve dollars all together. But Damion insisted on giving me a quarter of our whole week's earnings.

"Really, Damion, I don't think I'm entitled to all this. I mean, there were only two days that I made any money. You should get a much bigger share."

"But you were my partner for the whole week," he pointed out. "Even if you didn't make that much at first, you were working for me."

"Well . . ."

He clasped my hand, put a wad of bills in it, and folded my fingers over the money.

He didn't let go of my hand.

"My little blushing peach," he began in his normal tone. But then his voice broke and he fixed his suddenly intense eyes on mine and growled, "Forget the fruit crap. Don't you know you're driving me out of my *tree?*"

"Me? *Me?*" I gasped. Stunned, I tried to back away from him on the couch where we sat, but he was still clutching my hand, so tightly now it was beginning to hurt.

"Right out of my tree," he repeated hoarsely.

I couldn't believe this was happening. For months I'd dreamed about Mr. Conrad saying these very words to me and finally someone was saying them and who did it turn out to be but *Damion Flamm*. Damion Flamm, who talked like

162

W. C. Fields and looked like an unmade bed and who had ten teeth too many and all the personality of a used car salesman.

Why did my parents pick this night of all nights to go to the movies?

"Damion, you're hurting my *hand!*"

He let go. I slid all the way to the other end of the couch. He slid after me.

"Where are your parents?" he asked urgently.

"They—they went to the movies."

"When will they be back?"

"M-m-momentarily." Lie! Not for *hours!*

I leaped up from the couch and stood defiantly in the exact center of the living room.

He came toward me.

"Damion, I am not driving you out of your tree," I said, as firmly as I could. "How could I possibly be? What have I *done?*"

"It's not what you've done," he said, his voice deep and husky. "It's what you *are.*"

"What *am* I?" I asked desperately, and immediately knew that was the wrong question.

His eyes got all soft and faraway and his lips twitched.

"You're Julie, Juliet—the only girl in the world like you—"

"Damion, that's—that's—of course I'm the only girl in the world like me!"

I was floundering, groping for words. If I managed to put together the right combination of words Damion would disappear. This whole evening would be erased. None of this would have ever happened.

"Would you like a Coke?" I asked weakly.

"Julie!" My name came out as one long, anguished howl.

I panicked. I couldn't make sense out of my thoughts. This boy was *suffering*. I was actually making Damion suffer. Nothing in life had prepared me for this moment—nothing like this ever happened to me before. I'm just not the type to drive men insane with passion. At least, I never *had* been.

Confused, I began to edge my way toward the dining room.

"Tea?" I offered stupidly.

"You," he said, and fixed his watery blue eyes on me. I was the mongoose being hypnotized by the snake prior to being swallowed whole.

He advanced.

I backed into the edge of the dining room table.

"Can I—is it all right if I kiss you?"

And all of a sudden I was in command of the situation. For in none of the innumerable variations I had played on this moment in fantasy did the man I dreamed about *ask* if he could kiss me. To ask meant that you were not sure; to ask meant that you had a suspicion that the other person found you less than irresistible. To ask meant that you weren't brave enough—or that your desire wasn't strong enough—to just plunge ahead and do it. To ask meant that I had a *choice*.

"No," I said. It came out kind of petulantly but

it had the right effect. Damion stopped dead in his tracks.

"No?" He looked shocked, as if he had written this script and what the hell was I doing throwing in all those ad libs?

"No, Damion, I'm sorry. And I want you to go home now." My voice was firmer, more confident. Inside I was still verging on a nervous breakdown, but I refused to give in to it.

"I'll give you back the money if you want."

"Money! What's money? Did you think I was trying to *buy* you?" His voice cracked.

"No," I said, softening a little. "No, of course I didn't think that." I wasn't exactly sure now whether I'd thought that or not, but it didn't matter.

He started to walk through the living room toward the hall.

He stopped and turned around.

"Maybe," he said a little too eagerly, "maybe I just sprung this on you too fast. Maybe if we got to know each other a little better—"

"No, Damion," I said gently. I wondered where I was getting my courage. "I don't think so. I know you well enough already. As a *friend*. And I hope we'll stay friends."

"Oh, sure, sure," he mumbled. "Friends."

He snatched his jacket off the banister of the stairs, where I had draped it, and let himself out. He closed the front door behind himself, very very gently.

I swallowed a few times and sank down on a

dining room chair. For a long time all I could do was shake my head in bewilderment and replay the whole crazy scene in my mind, over and over again.

Finally I stumbled upstairs to my room. I leaned on my dresser and gazed into the mirror. Scrutinizing my reflection, I tried to find something there that I'd never seen before, a sudden blossoming of great beauty, a sultry look in the eyes, moist, inviting lips—*something* to account for my sudden irresistibility.

I looked just the same. A little pale, perhaps, a lot more serious in expression than usual, but the same basic person gazed back at me from the mirror that evening as had that morning. Attractive enough, but certainly not overwhelming.

Having found no clue to solve the mystery, I hurried to the phone to call Nat and Isobel before I forgot any of the details.

Anyway, I told myself as I dialed Natalie's number, that's the last I'll see of Damion Flamm.

That was *not* the last I saw of Damion Flamm. In fact, Monday morning as I emerged from the bus, I found him waiting for me with my shopping bag as if nothing had ever happened to change things.

Natalie giggled. Isobel clamped her lips together, waggled her fingers at me cheerily and strolled away, leaving me face to face with what I feared might be a Broken Man.

"So, ready to go to work?" he asked brightly.

"You still—"

"Friends, right? Why not business partners too?"

He put the shopping bag down on the ground at my feet. "Look, strictly business, okay? We might as well be sensible about this."

"Sensible." I nodded my head vigorously. "Oh, sure, sensible."

"Great. Great. Now, I managed to get hold—"

"Damion Flamm?"

Two men, one in a brown suit and one in a raincoat materialized behind us. One wore a hat. One didn't. I'd never seen either of them before.

"Are you Damion Flamm?" the hatless one said.

"Yeah," Damion replied. His lip twitched.

They both took wallets out of their pockets and showed Damion something.

My mouth opened wide and I felt my knees threaten to give way. I wanted to move, I wanted desperately to be able to move, so I could just sort of walk casually away from this, just sort of amble toward the main door of the school and be swallowed up in the crowd.

But I couldn't move. I was frozen where I stood.

"Will you come with us please?" one of them asked. "We'd like to ask you a few questions."

Damion's face went white. He struggled to keep his cool.

"This girl," he said suddenly, shrilly, "knows nothing." He threw his arm around my shoulders protectively, as if to show the plainclothesmen we were barely acquainted.

"Oh, God," I muttered.

"Is this your bag, Miss?" He pointed to the shopping bag Damion had dropped at my feet.

"I—I—" My throat closed. My mouth stayed open, I gasped for air like a fish, but no words would come out. I'm in trouble, I thought wildly. I'm in trouble, I'm in trouble, I'm—

"Innocent as a newborn *child*," Damion cried.

"Will you come with us, Miss?"

How can I go with them if I can't move? They won't *carry* me, will they? How many people are watching this? They won't *drag* me, will they? If I actually, physically *can't move*, what will they do to me?

". . . my rights," Damion was jabbering. "You have to read me my rights."

"We're not arresting you," the man said mildly. "We only have to read you your rights when we're arresting you. All we're asking you for is a little cooperation."

I was moving. A helpful hand at my elbow, and I was moving. One foot stumbled in front of the other until I reached the unmarked car. I was helped into the back seat.

Dazed, I noticed nothing more until I found myself walking once again, out of the car, into the precinct house.

". . . allowed one phone call!" Damion was insisting. "I know my rights!"

"I'll bet you do," said the uniformed cop at the desk.

"Look, you can make six phone calls, ten phone calls," the plainclothesman said irritably. "I don't care, you can call up the whole world—*after* we talk." He led Damion off into a room somewhere and closed the door.

The detective who'd been wearing the hat, but who had taken it off at some point, led me down the hall into another room. It was just an office. There was a woman typing and a man in shirtsleeves working at a desk.

"I didn't see your identification," I remembered suddenly. "How do I know you're a cop?"

The woman who was typing looked up at me strangely. She checked her chest and arms, as if to reassure herself that her blue uniform was indeed on, then exchanged shrugs with the guy in shirtsleeves.

"Here." An identification card was flashed in front of me. Sergeant Wallace. Through some sort of glaze that was over my eyes I dimly made out that his first name was Algernon.

They probably call him Al, I thought. Or Algie. That's seaweed. They probably don't call him that. Al is probably what they—

"What's your name?"

"Julie Howe."

"Julie, what is your relationship with Damion Flamm?"

"Relationship?" Why, we were friends, that's

all. Just friends. Hadn't we firmly established that on Friday? Friends.

"How well do you know him?"

"I—I—" How do you answer a question like that?

"Did you ever see him selling things? Around the school?"

"Yes."

"Does he do this regularly, or just once in a while?"

"Pretty regularly." I couldn't speak above a whisper.

"How regularly?"

"Well, you know—regularly."

"Once a week? Twice a week?"

"Five times," I choked.

"He's done it five times?"

"Five times a week," I wailed.

"You mean, every day."

"When there's school," I said miserably. "Not on Saturdays or Sundays."

"And you?"

I didn't know what he meant. I looked at him blankly. I tried to hold back the tears and failed.

"Do you do any selling?"

"Five times," I confessed, my voice almost a shriek. "But why are you—we didn't do anything illegal—"

He pushed a box of Kleenex toward me.

"A week?"

"What? No, no all together five times!"

"Where'd he get the stuff to sell?"

"I don't know!" I cried. "I have no idea."

"Didn't he tell you?"

"No, he never told me. He said he knew a guy. He said not to worry about it, that that was his worry."

I yanked tissues out of the box wildly. That *creep,* I thought, that creep, Damion. He tells me he loves me and gives me hot looseleaf paper to peddle. The stuff *was* stolen. All the while he's chuckling over hot paperclips and they really *were* hot.

"And you never had any idea where the stuff came from?"

"No!"

The man who had taken Damion away stuck his head in the door and gestured to Sergeant Wallace. They spoke softly for a minute, then Sergeant Wallace came back to me.

"All right," he said. "You can go."

"What?" I looked up at him, uncertain of what he was saying.

"You can go. We have nothing on you and the kid backs up your story."

I closed my eyes and took a deep breath.

"I'll have someone drive you back to school."

"What's going to happen to Damion?" I asked hoarsely.

"That depends," he said. He refused to be any more explicit. "You know, this doesn't go on a record or anything," he volunteered. "I didn't even write your name down anywhere. And you were very cooperative."

"Thank you," I managed.

He drove me back to school himself in the same unmarked car.

"I'm going to need," I told him tearfully, "a late pass."

Damion was put on probation. He admitted that he suspected that the guy who was supplying him with all that stuff was ripping off the company where he worked, but he insisted that he never knew for *sure*. And like me, he hadn't bothered to inquire too closely. Somehow, no one ever asked Damion about watches, and as far as I know, Damion never mentioned watches again.

From then on I did all my shopping at the Student Store.

They were usually out of most of the stuff I needed.

11. DEMONSTRATIONS OF AFFECTION, SUCH AS HAND-HOLDING, ETC., ARE INAPPROPRIATE IN A SCHOOL ATMOSPHERE AND ARE VIGOROUSLY DISCOURAGED.

Dear Family,

Everything is coming along nicely for a change. I am running A's in Poli Sci, History and Geology and a B in English Lit Survey. And either a C or B in Psych, I'm not sure which. It all depends on how the prof feels about you at the moment.

Right now he seems to think I tend toward the frivolous, simply because I named my white rat Maisie and tied a ribbon around her neck, instead of giving her a letter name, like Rat Q.

I tried to tell him that this sort of personal attention would motivate Maisie more to learn to run her maze and find her food pellets, but he didn't seem impressed. See, he's more used to studying rats and applying their behavior characteristics to people than he is to studying people and applying *their* behavior characteristics to rats.

This may seem like a small difference of approach to you, but believe me, it is symptomatic of the great disparity in outlook between us. Anyway, only time will tell.

I'm convinced that Maisie, because of all this personal attention, will learn to run her maze faster than any of the other rats; if the prof is big enough to admit I'm right, I ought to get a B. If he feels I've acted like a smartass and shown him up, I'll get a C, despite [or because of] the fact that my hypothesis will have proved right.

I met this really terrific girl, Delores Chin. She plans to be a vet and she's a wonder with animals. When she finishes here at Dodd [two more years] she's going to take the veterinary science program at Cornell. She's already a whiz at things like fixing broken wings and nursing sick chickens back to health. Her dorm room is always filled with convalescent birds; I don't know where she finds them all.

She had a roommate, but the roommate requested a room change, because she said all the clucking and cheeping kept her from studying, and when Delores brought home a baby owl and began to teach it to catch its own prey, the roommate said that was the last straw.

Anyway, I may come home for a weekend

soon and I'll try and get Delores to come with me. She won't leave her patients, though, so we'll probably have to bring them with us. [Try and keep calm, Mom. They're all mostly in shoeboxes and things. Except for the owl, of course.]

Marlene and Carlos were arrested a couple of weeks ago for lying down in front of a former Head Start Center that's being torn down for phone company computer offices. They threw themselves right in the path of the bulldozer and were busted for disturbing the peace. Since then Marlene has been wearing Carlos's Sam Browne belt over her T-shirt and she's going to Argentina with him for the summer.

Isn't life strange?

That seems to be all the news from here. Hope you're all well.

Love,
Gabe

Ever since the first meeting of the Explorers' Club I had been aware that Gary Gordon was aware of me. That sounds like a funny way to put it; there was really nothing to go on but the fact that he drove me to and from every meeting, sat next to me at every meeting, and seemed to enjoy joking with me in homeroom.

It all seemed terribly platonic and during the time when Mr. Conrad was the only male who occupied my waking—and sleeping—thoughts I didn't pay much attention to the question of whether Gary was too shy to actually ask me out or just not interested in me as anything other than a friend. At that point, I really didn't care.

After I emerged from the shadow of my hopeless affair, I began to wonder about Gary. He watched me at Explorers' meetings. I mean, when I talked, he *watched* me, with a certain intensity that the other people who listened while I talked just didn't show.

And after the meetings, when he was giving rides home to other people, he always drove me home last, even when it was out of his way.

I began to wonder about the whole thing. If he did like me, why didn't he ask me out to the movies or something, alone? And if he just wanted to be friends, well, why didn't he treat me like any of his other friends? Why didn't he ever sit next to someone else at the Explorers' Club? Why did he always drive me home last?

And, on the other hand again, why didn't he say or do something that could only be said and done alone, those times when we were alone in his car?

Once I started to think about this, it really began to bug me. I kept going over the same arguments in my mind and kept returning to the same place I'd started, namely, I couldn't figure out what—if anything—Gary felt about me.

So I tried to figure out what—if anything—I felt about him. Oddly enough, I couldn't imagine him suddenly fixing me with a passionate stare, as Damion Flamm had, and announcing that I was driving him out of his tree. Although I could and did fantasize Mr. Conrad saying and doing all kinds of marvelous things, my otherwise fertile imagination dried up when faced with the enigma of Gary Gordon.

Did I like him?

Well, sure. What was not to like? He was nice, intelligent, good-looking, had a sense of humor and was unaggressively masculine.

But did I *like* him?

And if I did, what could I do about it anyway?

Some girls, feeling that it was as reasonable for a girl to ask a boy out as vice-versa, were able to just go up to a fellow they thought they'd like to go out with and ask him. Isobel did that and with great success. She said boys were even shyer than girls in some cases and were greatly relieved not to have to run the risk of asking a girl out and being rejected.

But I couldn't bring myself to do that. (If I had, perhaps the whole saga of Mr. Conrad would have had a different ending.) I didn't want to face the possibility of being rejected myself, and I simply couldn't work up the nerve to ask a boy to take me out.

Even if I'd been sure I wanted Gary Gordon to take me out.

It was at just this point in my confusion that Tony Lambert and Joan Slater broke up and the Explorers' Club gave an April Fool party.

The plans for the party were a big secret,

closely guarded by the party committee, which consisted of Tony and Joan (whose parting, apparently, had been amicable), Gary and Barbara Lipton. The only thing the other members knew was that we were to expect quite a change from the normal Explorers' "atmosphere."

The whole thing was very intriguing and no matter how I nagged Gary to even give me a hint of what the party was going to be like, he remained tight-lipped and mysterious about it, right up to April 1.

On the night of the party Gary came to drive me over. Despite the fact that he was supposed to be at Joan's early to help with the preparations, I really was not all that surprised to find him at our front door offering me a ride.

"We got everything done already," he explained as we went out to the car. "And I thought you might need a lift."

We were halfway to Joan's house when Gary suddenly said, "You know, we never get a chance to talk very much."

Startled, I said the only thing that I could think of.

"Gary, we talk all the time."

"Yeah, I know, but I mean *really* talk."

I shifted nervously in my seat. I knew what he meant and I suspected that at last he was going to make a move, but I wasn't all that eager, at this very moment, to have him make it. After all, if we hadn't talked before, it wasn't because we didn't have the opportunity. Goodness, we were alone together at least in the car, every Wednesday. If he'd been that anxious to talk, why hadn't he done so before?

The truth was that Tony Lambert was not going with Joan Slater any more . . . At the first Explorers' meeting I had ever gone to I'd been certain Tony was interested in me, though nothing ever came of it. Now, however, he was available and who knew what might happen at the party tonight?

It's not wise to foreclose all your options, I told myself judiciously.

The fact was, the thought of being kissed by Tony—or even having Tony's arm draped casually around my shoulders, as I had so often seen him with Joan—made my heart flutter and my skin prickle just the way Mr. Conrad had. I'd been sitting next to Gary for weeks, yet I was still wondering how I felt about him.

Emotion-wise, it was No Contest.

I didn't say anything because all the things I could think of to say would lead him into explaining what was on his mind, and I didn't want that just now. So I didn't try to make it any easier for him by saying something like, "What would you like to talk about?" or "Okay, let's *really* talk."

I guess I didn't make it any harder for him either, because a moment later he said, "Sometimes you seem pretty preoccupied. You know, you put on this good-humored, carefree act, but underneath it all there's a part of you you don't let other people see. And you have things on your mind that you don't tell anyone about."

This whole line of conversation made me edgy. I wasn't really all that aware of putting on a ho, ho, ho act, but it was true that I kept certain worries to myself. I had told absolutely no one, not even Natalie (Isobel, of course I'd never tell) about Mr. Conrad, but then, everyone has a private side and it's kind of uncomfortable to have someone pointing out that they notice it. The whole point of a private side is privacy, after all. If I told my troubles to everyone, everyone would get sick and tired of listening to me.

I thought of all these things but said none of them to Gary. I didn't want to tell him he was right and I didn't want to prolong this disconcerting analysis of Me.

But I couldn't help thinking that he had put a lot of time into observing me and trying to figure me out. Which, if I hadn't guessed by now, would have tipped me off to how he felt about me.

"Right now," he said abruptly, "you're closing up. I can feel it. You're closing yourself off from me."

"Well, Gary," I said defensively, "I just want to get in a party mood. This is all too heavy for me right now. We're going to a party to have fun and fool around, and my mind just isn't tuned in to a big psychological session tonight."

"Click," he said. "Closed."

He was right, of course.

Luckily we were at Joan's house.

"The whole place looks dark," I said as we walked up the front steps. "If I weren't with you, I'd think I had the wrong night."

"It *is* dark; part of the atmosphere."

He rang the bell.

The door opened slowly and Joan, holding a candelabra and grinning from ear to ear said, "Welcome . . . to the world of the Unexplained." She tried to say it in a deep, eerie voice, but ended up giggling.

"I *gotta* stop breaking up when I say that," she told Gary. "It ruins the whole atmosphere."

"That's okay," I said, peering down the dark hall. "If you make things any scarier I might just go home."

"You ain't seen nothin' yet," she assured me, pulling me inside and shutting the door behind us. "Follow me. Gary, you go first, otherwise Julie won't get the full impact."

Gary hurried off down the hall and disappeared.

Then Joan led the way, the candles flickering to barely light our path and creating shadows that lurked along the hall. There were posters on the walls on both sides of the narrow passage, but I could only catch glimpses of them as we went by. There was a skull, a very old and melodramatic-looking ad for a hypnotist with a mustache, cape and violently magnetic eyes, and various other decorations dealing with one or another occult "science."

"Watch the steps," Joan said as we started down to the basement. There was no light on the stairs either, the only illumination still coming from Joan's candles. I gripped the banister and went down the steps very carefully.

I could hear noise in the basement, ordinary party noise—people talking, eating, laughing—which dispelled some of the eeriness. I felt relieved. It's silly to be so on edge, I told myself. It's just a party, and this is all just a big joke anyway.

Joan led me into a totally dark room. The sound of laughter and chattering was all around me but as Joan held the candelabra forward, I could see that the room was absolutely empty.

"But—but—I hear them! They're right here!" I looked around wildly, trying to spot people crouching in corners or underneath chairs, but there was no one there, no matter what my ears told me.

"Isn't that odd?" Joan said thoughtfully.

It was a joke of course, some sort of April Fool gag, but I couldn't help reacting. I actually wanted to run out of that very weird room.

"Oh, there goes the bell," Joan said. "I have to go up and let them in. Listen, why don't you try that door over there, and see if there's anyone in the next room?"

She turned, and taking the only light in the room with her, went back up the stairs.

In complete blackness, and near panic, I made my way over to where the door was, or where I thought I remembered it was. I had to feel along the wall for a while until my fingers found the knob, and then I hesitated before turning it. It was pitch black in here, but who knew what was in *there?*

Finally I couldn't stand waiting there blindly any more. I turned the knob.

"We thought you'd never get here!" Tony shouted jovially.

I nearly collapsed on the threshold. The room, lit by candles, was the actual area of the party, and while there were several people already there, it didn't sound at all like the party I'd heard in the other room.

"What took you so long?" Tony asked.

I tried to regain what little composure I had. It didn't help to notice that Gary, who was seated to the left of the door, was gazing at me.

"How did you do that?" I asked weakly. "With the noise in there?"

"Ah, but this is the world of the Unexplained," Tony said smoothly. "Where all things are possible and nothing is what it seems."

He reached around me to close the door, so the next person in would have the same experience I had. Instead of moving aside and making my way toward the other people in the room, I just stood there, enjoying him so close to me.

"Come have something to eat," he said, as I smiled up at him, practically demanding that he notice me. "We really blew the treasury on this."

He put his hand at my back and steered me toward a table laden with cold cuts, bread, salads and snack-type stuff. I was not at all hungry and wished the walk to the table had been longer, even though I could feel Gary's eyes practically burning a hole in the back of my neck.

I felt a distinct letdown when Tony dropped his hand.

"What a spread," I said admiringly.

"Well, we want you to keep your strength up," Tony smiled.

"Will I need it?" I asked, wide-eyed.

"You might." His grin was mildly devilish.

A few more white faces appeared at the door and Tony went off to greet them. Left alone, I scooped up a couple of potato chips and looked around. Consuela was in one corner with Albert, who was not a member of the Explorers and whom I hadn't seen at all since my retreat from the *Taproots* office. I guessed he was her date. A little apart from them Barbara Lipton, George, and Bert Brady were clustered together. George and Barbara called out, "Hi," and I wiggled my fingers at them.

Gary was still seated near the door, alone.

I didn't want to put myself in a position of having to stay with him through the whole party, but he was the best friend I had there, and there was no graceful way of avoiding him.

I strolled over to the couch.

"Hey, can I make you a sandwich or something?" I asked, in a suitably friendly voice. It was as if I could escape committing myself by not sitting right down or something.

He looked up at me curiously.

"I can make my own sandwich if I want one. Sit down and relax."

"How can you relax in this place?" I joked.

Relaxation was out of the question, but the dim room was not the reason.

"I mean, you want us to be at least a *little* scared, isn't that the whole point?"

"More or less," Gary said indifferently. "Though by now I've just about forgotten what the whole point is."

"I guess just to have a good time and do something different."

He looked away from me and I followed his gaze to where Tony was standing, leaning idly against the door, waiting for the next contingent of mystified guests. My eyes met Tony's and I realized he'd been watching me as I'd talked with Gary.

I smiled gently, almost secretively at him, completely forgetting to worry about whether or not Gary would notice. Tony smiled back knowingly, then looked away.

I closed my eyes for a moment and tried to suppress the thrill of realization that it was going to happen. I knew it, I just knew for certain after that wordless communication, that something was brewing between Tony and me.

What I wanted to do right then was to jump up and whirl around the room a few times, but what I did was to open my eyes and lean back, catlike and content, against the sofa.

I was confident, feminine and irresistible. I tasted a tantalizing power as I realized that the boy I had a crush on had fallen under my spell and the boy who had a crush on me was jealous.

It was a glorious feeling and utterly new to me.

I sat there and smiled benevolently at the world.

Joan explained that the theme of the party was the occult experience, and while we wouldn't exactly explore the unknown, as we would if this were an ordinary Explorers' meeting, we would sample and experience various phases of it.

"So let me introduce first, The Great Torolino, Hypnotist Extraordinaire!"

The door leading from the empty room was flung open and in strode a man in a black cape, top hat and dress suit. He doffed his hat, bowed low before us and waited for applause.

We applauded.

"Did you pay him?" I asked Gary in a whisper.

"Shh!"

I didn't recognize him, but he might have been someone from school, with makeup on. Otherwise, how could the Explorers have afforded all this?

"I would like to demonstrate to you some of the strange effects of hypnotism on human subjects," he said, with a slight accent which I couldn't place. He looked sort of like the hypnotist on the poster in the hall.

"I need a volunteer."

Joan volunteered. He had her sit on a chair in the center of the room.

He waved a pocket watch on a chain in front of her and commanded her to sleep. Her eyelids lowered and her head drooped forward. Soon she was breathing deeply.

"You will obey my every command. I want you to go over to the person you love most in this room, and give that person a kiss."

Was she faking? I didn't believe she was really hypnotized, especially since she'd planned the whole thing, but we all watched, hypnotized ourselves, as Joan walked over to her best friend, Dana Bergman, and kissed her on the cheek,

Everybody laughed and clapped and I glanced over toward Tony, wondering if he thought she'd kiss him, even though they had broken up. But no, he was probably in on the whole thing anyway.

The Great Torolino "woke" Joan up and asked for another volunteer.

This time, though several hands went up, he picked Gary.

I hoped that he wouldn't repeat the stunt.

The hypnotist didn't use the watch on Gary, but just talked softly to him, telling him to relax. Without the watch it seemed a lot less theatrical than Joan's trance, and when Torolino told Gary he wouldn't be able to lift his arm no matter how he tried, I almost believed that Gary was really hypnotized. He couldn't lift his arm, although he was obviously straining to, and the look on his face was one of genuine frustration.

"Why don't you try that with someone else?" Con demanded. "Everyone you're picking was on the party committee."

"Would you like to try it?" the Great Torolino asked graciously.

Con hesitated only a moment.

"Sure."

He woke Gary and gestured for Con to come to the middle of the room and sit in the chair. Of all the people in the room to hypnotize, I was sure Con must be the hardest to put in a "trance." But in a matter of minutes, Torolino repeated exactly the same suggestion that he'd given Gary, and, amazingly, Con was just as incapable of lifting her arm as Gary had been.

Now, of course, no one could be sure whether or not Torolino was actually hypnotizing people, or if he was just hypnotizing some people and had worked out an act with others. It was really mystifying.

"And now," he said, after rousing Con, "we're going to try something a little different. It is my belief that all of us have great, untapped powers of ESP that we never use, and that we are not even aware we possess. What I'm going to do is to hypnotize one of you and keep you in the trance state while I instruct you to release those powers and to use them to predict the future."

He asked Tony to be the subject and I was sure that we were going to see another pre-planned act, but he put him under the same way he'd hypnotized Con and Gary, so I wasn't at all certain what was real and what wasn't anymore.

"You're to stay in this state of consciousness,"

188

Torolino was saying, "and allow your sixth sense to function unhampered, until I instruct you to awaken. You will go into the next room and as each person here comes in to you, you will tell them what you see in their future. Do you understand?"

Tony nodded.

There was a great buzzing of anticipation. Even if it was all fixed, who can resist having their fortune told? And this was the most unusual fortune-telling gimmick I'd ever heard of.

Tony was led into the next room with a candelabra and seated behind a small table. Everyone clustered at the door, everyone eager to be the first to have his fortune told.

"One at a time," Torolino said, "and close the door behind you so the subject can fully concentrate on his predictions."

One by one they filed in to see Tony and as each person came out those still in line clustered around him to hear what Tony had said.

The predictions seemed to be fairly routine, based pretty much on the type of person whose fortune was being read. Con was told she'd be jailed three times before she was twenty, but would marry and have two children and live in the suburbs before she was thirty.

Gary didn't get in line to have his reading, but I did.

I tried to imagine what Tony would say to me when we were alone, and wondered whether he were really hypnotized, or what.

The Great Torolino made himself a pastrami sandwich.

It was finally my turn to go in.

The room was quite dim, being only candlelit, and Tony did not see that it was me until I sat down at the little table opposite him.

"Well," he said softly. "Well, now . . ."

He stood up and came around behind my chair. He put his hands on my shoulders.

"What are you doing?" I asked nervously.

"I have to get close to you for the vibrations to come through," he replied, sounding very reasonable. "You want to find out what life holds for you, don't you?"

"Within reason," I squeaked, as his hands caressed my shoulders. If I hadn't been sitting down, I would have had to. My breathing sounded funny, and I had to clutch my fingers together to keep my hands from trembling.

I was torn between wishing he'd stop, so I could get my breath again, and wishing he'd never stop, and we would just stay here together forever.

"What do I see in your future?" he mused, his hand now on the back of my neck.

At that moment I really didn't give a hoot for what the future held, considering that the present was more than I could handle, but if Tony was aware of the effect he was having on my nervous system, he didn't let on.

"As far as the very immediate future," he said

softly, "you will not leave the party with the same person you came in with."

My heart pounded as I realized that meant Tony was planning to take me home.

"And after that, you will find a new person in your life, a person who's very interested in you . . ."

A hideous thought struck me. Tony was certainly not hypnotized, this whole thing was a set-up, just for entertainment at the party, and today *was* April Fool's Day.

I let the idea horrify me for a moment, but then told myself that Tony was not cruel, that our eyes *had* met with romantic conspiratorialness not a half hour before, and *that* had surely not been an April Fool joke.

"You'll see a lot of this person," Tony went on. He returned to the other side of the table. I exhaled, possibly for the first time in a couple of minutes, and unclenched my hands.

"What does this person look like?" I whispered.

His eyes held mine for a long moment. He didn't answer.

I shifted uncomfortably in the chair, waiting for him to say something else. Finally I stood up.

"Is the reading over?" I could barely get the words out.

He nodded gravely.

I walked to the door, painfully conscious of his eyes following me.

I kept expecting him to say something else, but he didn't, and I stumbled into the next room and was immediately surrounded by people demanding to know what Tony had predicted for me.

I was still in a fog, and the questioning faces just blended together into a mass of fuzzy features. The only thing I could see clearly was Gary, sitting off on one side of the room, with a sober expression on his face.

"What did he tell you? What did he *say?*"

"Not too much."

"You were in there a long time," George pointed out.

"Was I?"

"Time sure flies when you're having fun," Barbara said drily.

"Come on, Julie, stop being so secretive. What's your future going to be like?"

"Nice," I gulped.

After all the fortunes were told, the Great Torolino stopped eating long enough to "wake" Tony from his trance. By this time I was much calmer, and felt that old confidence returning. The Great Torolino was thanked, applauded, and ushered out. He was still clutching a huge sandwich to his white-shirted chest.

Joan disappeared for a few minutes, then returned with a woman in a flowered print dress and fringed shawl who looked rather bewildered. She was probably just trying to adjust her eyes to the dimness of the room.

"This is Mrs. Briggs," Joan announced. "Mrs. Briggs is one of the foremost experts in the field of graphology. Barbara is handing out pencils and paper and I want you all to write the Pledge of Allegiance on them in your normal, everyday handwriting. I'm sure none of you have ever met Mrs. Briggs and she doesn't know any of us. But you're going to be amazed at how much your handwriting reveals about you, when Mrs. Briggs analyzes it and tells you about your personality."

Tony ambled over to where I was standing, near the food.

"Where did you *get* these people?" I asked.

"Having a good time?"

"Terrific. I don't know how you did it."

"As long as you're enjoying yourself."

"Oh, I definitely am." I smiled. I felt utterly adorable.

Mrs. Briggs worked with everyone watching, which was a lot of fun. And she was pretty good, too. She told Joan that she was an achiever, good at many things. She said that Con was highly emotional and tended to overreact in stress situations, but could channel her energy to good causes.

I listened intently as she analyzed Tony as "self-confident, sometimes verging on conceited." Everyone jeered at that, but Tony simply smiled confidently. Gary was told that he was intelligent, but somewhat secretive and introverted. "He keeps his feelings to himself," was the way Mrs. Briggs put it.

I found that funny, considering that Gary had said practically the same thing about me.

"Takes one to know one," I teased as I strolled past him to take my turn with Mrs. Briggs. He scowled.

"You are intelligent and creative," Mrs. Briggs told me.

I beamed.

"But immature."

I frowned. Everyone else thought it was pretty funny.

"You still need to develop—"

"Oh, I don't know," Tony interrupted. "She seems pretty well-developed already."

It's a good thing I'm not a blusher.

"That's not what I meant," Mrs. Briggs said sternly. "I meant that without discipline and maturity, your creative abilities may remain unfocused and vague. You may dissipate them by going off in all directions at once, instead of concentrating on doing one thing well."

I nodded attentively, although I didn't really see myself as that sort of person. Of course, that might have been because I was too immature to recognize it.

"*Now* I remember you," Albert said, after Mrs. Briggs went on to another reading.

Oh dear. I was sure the whole *Taproots* thing had been long forgotten.

"You do?"

"The girl with the poem. How come you never brought us back that poem?"

"Oh, I just decided it wasn't good enough to print," I said, which was certainly true.

"But we thought it was," Albert objected. "You really should let me make editorial decisions like that."

"Frankly," I said, "I thought the other stuff I'd showed you was much better, and I only wrote that poem because I knew it was the sort of thing you wanted."

"Well it *was*. It was a good poem."

I shrugged. "That's one person's opinion."

Albert scrutinized my face.

"That handwriting expert is right," he decided.

"You mean about my being creative?"

"No," he replied. "About your being immature."

After Mrs. Briggs left, the party just drifted along on its own for a while, like most other parties, with records and dancing and general socializing. Tony danced with me once. Gary didn't dance at all. At least he'd finally stopped his solitary brooding and was deep in a conversation with George and Dana.

Joan went around telling us there was to have been a magician, but he'd just called to say he was suffering from a stomach virus and could not venture more than five paces away from his bathroom.

It was pretty late by this time anyway, and everyone agreed that the party had been fun even without the magician.

People began to leave.

"Come on," said Tony, taking my arm. "I'll

drive you home. Anyone else need a ride?" he offered.

Gary frowned at me. I smiled weakly and looked away. After all, he wasn't my date. He'd never asked me out, and he'd just brought me to the party as a friend. There was no reason why I shouldn't let Tony drive me home.

Barbara Lipton and Bert Brady accepted the ride and we piled into Tony's car. After he'd driven both of them home I started to tell him how to get to my house.

"There's no rush, is there?" he asked easily. "You won't turn into a pumpkin or anything?"

He drove down a dark side street and pulled over to the curb.

"Where are we?" I asked nervously, as if it made any difference.

"Does it matter?"

He turned off the motor. The better to hear the wild beating of my heart. Surely he could hear it; it seemed deafening.

I forced myself to stop trembling as he leaned over and began to idly stroke my hair.

"All night I've waited to be alone with you," he said softly.

Before I could say anything, even if I had been able to think of anything to say, he pulled me to him, caressed my cheek with one hand, and kissed me on the lips.

When he let go of me I sank limply back against the seat, no longer able to control my ragged breathing or the trembling that threatened to become a permanent condition whenever I was near him.

For a moment I was too shaken to move. He started to reach for me again and instinctively I grabbed his hands in mine and held them tightly.

"T-Tony," I stammered. "I don't even *know* you."

He leaned back and grinned at me. "That's not true. You've known me for months."

I let go of his hands. "But—I mean, we never went out or anything."

"But you know I like you," he said, his voice low and persuasive.

"I didn't know," I said desperately. "I mean, this is too sudden—you—you're—I really don't think we—"

I didn't know what I thought. I wanted him to kiss me again and I hoped he wouldn't. I was too confused by my feelings to really think much at all.

He put his fingers on my lips, and I suddenly felt so weak that I let my eyes close because even keeping them open was a strain.

He kissed me again. My head was pressed against the front seat, which was as far back from Tony as I could get. Of all the jumble of sensations that flooded me, for some reason the most predominant one was a strange sensation of drowning.

When he finally let me go and I opened my eyes, I found him looking at me with an expression of mild amusement.

"Don't you like to be kissed?"

How could I answer that?

"Do you want me to take you home?"

I looked at him helplessly. How did I know what I wanted?

"I wish you'd say something."

"I don't know what to say," I murmured.

He turned the ignition on.

I was furious at myself. He was angry, upset, convinced I'd rejected him. The truth was that the speed at which my wishes were coming true dizzied me. It was all happening too fast, giving me no time to sort out my thoughts or measure my responses.

It's one thing to play the game of secret flirting across a crowded room, and another thing entirely to be alone in a car with a boy who is obviously a champion at other games whose rules you haven't even learned yet.

In a word, I was *scared*.

Tony drove me directly home. The only conversation we exchanged was when he asked for directions to my house, and I gave them.

"Here we are," he said, pulling into the driveway. He didn't turn the motor off.

"Tony? Would you like to come in for a Coke, or some coffee or something?"

"No thanks. I'll just be getting on home."

He got out of the car and came around to open the door for me. He walked me to my front door.

I blurted it out very quickly, before I could lose my nerve.

"Tony, I don't want you to think I don't like you."

"You just don't want me kissing you."

"It's not that. If we'd gone out a couple of times, if I'd gotten to know you a little better—"

"You like things all formalized and traditional," he declared, with a trace of scorn in his voice. "You don't go for the spontaneity of two people with normal impulses. You can only handle conformist courtship rituals."

"Well, there's a lot to be said for tradition." I didn't sound terribly convincing.

"Look, don't worry about it. You're still young, you have a lot of growing up to do yet, you're probably not ready to—"

"I'm getting a little tired of everybody telling me how immature I am!"

It was ridiculous. He was a senior and I was a sophomore. "You're only two years older than me!"

"Practically three," he said, "and it makes a big difference at your age."

That did it.

"Good night," I said coldly. "Thanks for driving me home."

"Listen, don't be angry just because I told you a few simple truths about yourself. Don't you want me to be open and honest with you?"

"Not if it means you're going to insult me. On the whole, I think I'd prefer a little hypocritical flattery."

I went inside and slammed the door behind me.

I resisted the impulse to peek out the front window to see if he would stand there on the doorstep, dazed, for a little while before leaving.

He couldn't have stood there too long, since I heard the car pulling out of the driveway barely a moment later.

I wished I could call Isobel, but it was much too late. I knew I had to talk to someone, to get another person's point of view on the whole bewildering experience. What was I so afraid of? Why had I acted like such a fumbling, inexperienced *baby?*

No matter how hard I tried to repress and ignore it, the unwelcome answer returned again and again.

I *was* fumbling and inexperienced.

I called Iz the next morning, early enough to wake her.

She sounded so sleepy that as I related the events of the night before, I kept saying, "Are you still there?" to make sure she hadn't dozed off while I talked.

"What's so terrible about being young?" she asked.

"Then you think I'm immature too?"

"*You* think so." Izzie yawned. "That's what counts."

"I don't know if I am or not."

"I wouldn't get so upset about it."

"I know you wouldn't. You don't confuse as easily as I do."

"You know what I think? I think that you're the type of person who doesn't want to jump right into a heavy relationship with another person; I think you're the kind of person that has to take her time with these things."

"That's practically the same thing Tony said."

Iz groaned a little. "I'm stretching," she explained.

"You know, it sounded like a putdown when he said it," I went on.

"Maybe you just got aggravated with all these people telling you you're immature. But for heaven's sakes, what's so terrible about being young? You're not going to stay young forever. You'll be old and decrepit before you know it."

"Gee, I feel better already."

"I have a way with words," Iz said modestly. "And I don't see what's so terrible about being scared either. Why shouldn't you have been nervous? It was a new situation and you weren't prepared for it."

"You wouldn't have been scared," I said glumly. "You would have known just how to handle it."

"So? I'm not you and you're not me. We're different. We react to things differently."

"I guess you're right. But Tony won't bother with me now."

"It's just as well," said Izzie carelessly. "He's probably just another pretty face."

The doorbell rang. I looked up at the clock and saw it was barely ten.

"Iz, someone's at the door. I'll call you later. I don't know if anyone else is up."

"At this hour? I should hope not."

I ran downstairs, as the bell rang for the third time. My parents weren't down yet, and I'd just thrown my robe over my nightgown.

It was Gary.

I clutched my robe around me and tried not to show my surprise.

"Did I wake you?" he asked.

"Oh, no, I was up. I just didn't get dressed yet."

What in the world was he doing here at this hour? What in the world was he doing here at *all*, after last night? And why did I suddenly find myself delighted to see him standing on my doorstep?

"I thought—I sort of wanted to talk to you."

"Well, come on in. Have you had breakfast?"

He came inside and shut the door.

"No. Have you?"

"Not yet. Should I make some eggs or something?"

He brightened. "Hey, listen, you want to go to the diner? We could have breakfast there."

"Yeah, that would be fun. Let me go get dressed."

I started up the stairs and he said, "Uh, Julie? If you and Tony—I mean, after last night I don't know what's—what I mean is, if everything's settled between you and Tony—"

"Everything's settled," I said, smiling at him. "And I *really* would like to have breakfast with you."

I ran upstairs to my room.

It was amazing, I thought, as I flung open drawers and raced to get dressed. Not five minutes ago I was confused and miserable, and here I was, singing as I pulled on my jeans.

So—Gary had taken quite some time before he decided that he really liked me. He too was the kind of person who couldn't just jump into a relationship. We were really very much alike.

I'd known him for as long as he'd known me, and yet even yesterday I wasn't sure how I felt about him. It wasn't so surprising then that he would take his time getting to know me better.

And that, after all, was just what I had tried to explain to Tony; and that was what Tony couldn't seem to understand.

So Gary and I were young. So what was so terrible about being young? It just meant we had plenty of time before we got old.

I scrawled a note for my parents and taped it on their bedroom door.

"Hope I didn't make you wait too long," I told Gary as I bounded down the stairs.

"What's the hurry?" His smile made me feel like singing again. "We've got all the time in the world."

ABOUT THE AUTHOR

ELLEN CONFORD is the author of many popular books that have established her as an award-winning writer for young readers. Some of her books have also been made into TV movies. She writes three to five hours a day—or ten pages, whichever comes first! Not only does she love writing and reading but also crossword puzzles and word games; Ms. Conford is a champion Scrabble player—the 1981 Champion of the Long Island Scrabble Club she belongs to, and was a semifinalist in the first U.S. Open Crossword Puzzle Championship. But besides words, she loves old movies, enjoys needlework, and collects cookbooks.

Ms. Conford went to school at Hofstra University and still enjoys taking classes when she has the time. She lives in Massapequa, Long Island, New York, with her husband who is a college professor, a college-age son, and a very lovable sheepdog.